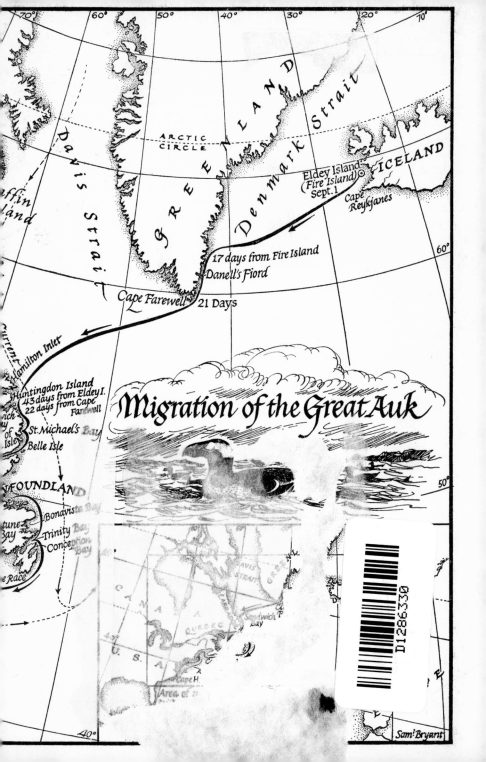

70° 60° 50° 40° 30° 20° 70°

G R E E N L A N D

Davis Strait

ARCTIC
CIRCLE

Denmark Strait

Eldey Island
(Fire Island)
Sept. 1

ICELAND

Cape
Reykjanes

17 days from Fire Island

Danell's Fiord

Cape Farewell — 21 Days

Hamilton Inlet

Huntingdon Island
43 days from Eldey I.
22 days from Cape
Farewell

St. Michael's Bay

Belle Isle

NEWFOUNDLAND

Bonavista Bay

Trinity Bay
Conception Bay

e Race

60°

50°

40°

Migration of the Great Auk

CANADA

DAVIS
STRAIT

GREEN

QUEBEC

Sandwich
Bay

U.S.A.

Cape H.
Area of 2.

Sam¹ Bryant

The Great Auk

The Great Auk

a novel by

ALLAN W. ECKERT

LITTLE, BROWN AND COMPANY • BOSTON • TORONTO

Published simultaneously in Canada
by Little, Brown & Company (Canada) Limited

PRINTED IN THE UNITED STATES OF AMERICA

For Joan — my beloved wife — whose love, faith and patience have never faltered

The Great Auk

I

ELDEY ISLAND loomed ahead of them like a gigantic red iceberg jutting from the frigid gray waters of the North Atlantic. Dimly in the haze behind it the swimmers could see the desolate coastline of southwestern Iceland.

The austere cliffs of the island were softened by the light of first sun, and the salt-slick of sea water on its lower surface turned soot-colored rock into a magical mirror which caught and reflected the early sun. At this time of day the island was no mere tangle of tumbled rock and cliff, but a vivid flashing fire rising mysteriously from the sea. Across that lower portion where the sea water never quite drained away before being replenished by another thunderous swell, it was red-orange. This brilliance quickly diminished to a dusky pink where the cliffs thrust above all but the highest droplets of exploding spray, and then even higher, toward the top, it deepened to a dull gray almost like smoke leaving the flaming base.

For the hardy sailors of Icelandic ports who plied these waters, the sight was familiar and forbidding. They called it Fire Island and respected it as a hazard not to be lightly or carelessly approached by any man. The reddish bulk — which gradually turned a uniform ominous gray-black as day progressed — was a natural warning beacon to steer clear of these dangerous waters with their treacherous undertows and rock walls, their rips and hidden reefs that could shear through or crush the toughest hull upon contact.

To that strangely half-submerged armada of huge birds surging toward it from the open sea to the west, however, it was a most welcome sight and marked the culmination of an incredible migratory swim that had commenced nearly three thousand miles away. There were more than eighty birds in this flock, and they spread out haphazardly in loose clusters which trailed behind the lead bird to a distance of nearly half a mile.

The great auks had come home.

Of the many species of birds which annually nested here on Eldey Island after lengthy spring migrations, the great auks were the only ones that did not arrive on wing. They were, in fact, the only flightless birds of the North Atlantic. Their tiny wings were not capable of raising the large bodies into the air. Yet, this was little handicap. These ridiculous flipperlike appendages — pumping in perfect harmony with the

vast splayed feet with their tough rubbery webbing —
could propel the birds on or beneath the billowing
ocean surface faster than six strong men could row
a dinghy.

When standing upright, the great auks considerably
resembled their husky cousins of the far Antarctic,
the penguins. A full thirty inches tall, even their dress
was similar to the penguins. Their heads, necks, backs
and wings were a deep glossy black, with the exception of a distinctive oval white spot between the beak
and each eye. Their undersides were a startling white
visible for miles when the birds stood high on the
cliffs of the islands like the one now before them.
The heavy, pointed beak was black in the males,
slightly yellowish in the females, streaked with gray,
somewhat thickened at the tip and incredibly strong.

The pace of this large raft of birds quickened as it
neared its destination, and miniature wakes spread out
behind each bird. Despite their unusual speed and
grace in the water, their swimming was odd and gave
the impression of being badly imbalanced. The large
hindquarters rode higher on the surface than the remainder of the bird's body. The massively muscled
legs were situated so near the tail that the pistonlike
strokes of the paddling feet cupping the water and
thrusting it behind shoved the breast portion of the
bird deeply into the water. The back sloped quite

sharply downward from the tail until just behind the head it was constantly awash. The streamlined neck and head rose from the surface like some weird beaked serpent and the thin wings pushed the water behind them with the balanced, powerful strokes of a master oarsman.

A particularly heavy swell raised the leading great auks high and the glistening white of their undersides flashed a shining greeting to the tens of thousands of varied sea birds standing sentinel on the tiny island as if in honor of this approaching flock — the last of the island's many migrants to arrive.

A raucous yet melodic thunder penetrated the early morning slash of gusty wind and the futile pounding of salt-heavy waves. The air became full of flying forms: the great auk's little cousin, the puffin, whose brilliantly colored parrotlike beak bubbled with a deep mirthful laughter as he swept past on rapidly beating wings; another cousin, the razor-billed auk, whose advantage over the great auks was the power of flight; the heavier, slower flight of the large eggbird or thick-billed murre, wildly crying *"Errrr! Errrr!"* from overhead; the direct graceful flight of the not much smaller sea pigeons or black guillemots as they arrowed past only scant inches above the water.

There, too, flew the large shearwaters and fulmars and skuas, while shoulder to shoulder in every conceivable niche of the island's rocky face stood the hook-beaked green and double-crested cormorants. Above them all, darting daintily and elegantly above the uppermost clefts were scores of storm petrels and snowy Iceland gulls. Miraculously, there were no collisions.

Late May is a beautiful time in most parts of the Northern Hemisphere, but on this chunk of barren rock it was not. Except for scattered greenish lichens and a struggling clump of coarse brown grass now and again in the looser stones of the island's surface, there was no trace of vegetation. In those lower rocky cavities that were constantly smashed by the high tides, quantities of ugly brownish-yellow seaweeds had been deposited by the waves and permeated the air with a faint odor of decomposition.

While from a distance Eldey Island seemed impenetrable by sea, in several places the rocky shore sloped with surprising gentleness into the water and these occasional landing points were surrounded by great black boulders that jutted through the foam-flecked surface. In some areas, however, the cliffs and promontories rose to a high, sheer, two hundred feet above the rumbling swells.

The raft of great auks slowed as it neared these wave-smashed rocky approaches to the island. Unskilled at walking, the landing operation was a tricky and dangerous business for them. One slight miscalculation might permit a wave to hurl a bird with devastating force against the unyielding rock. The birds milled about excitedly as the rear of the flock closed ranks and mingled with the van.

The leader of the multitude, a large male bird, approached an area where a vast slab of toppled rock planed gently into the sea. Its surface was slick with the constant scouring action of the water, but it seemed the most reasonable place to attempt a landing. The lead bird swam back and forth in front of this shelf, his head cocked gravely to one side as if estimating the ebb and flow fluctuations of the waves and swells, the angle of the rock's elevation from the water and other factors necessary to effect the landing. Twice he submerged with scarcely a ripple and flashed through the water with the ease and speed of a fish, scanning the subsurface features of the problem.

Satisfied, he surfaced, shook his head — and a gravelly squawk erupted from his throat, louder and deeper than any other of the thousands of bird voices about them, unmistakable in its clarity, undeniable in its authority.

Expertly the great auk permitted a large swell to carry him far onto the rock, and when the water receded the great flat feet firmly gripped the surface of the slick rock and the bird waddled forward toward higher and more level ground. The others followed without delay. Each swell was neatly reckoned for strength and distance and permitted to carry four or six or ten of the birds to the rock surface in the same manner. Within minutes the entire congregation stood in a screeching, self-congratulatory cluster on a relatively flat surface a score of feet above the high-water mark.

For a short time there seemed to be some confusion, a marked reluctance to separate as individuals after their long migration as a unit under controlled leadership. But this mood evaporated swiftly and the birds began waddling off in various directions, some only to turn and thrust themselves back into the sea.

Afloat, the great auks were graceful and majestic. Their swimming prowess — whether atop the water surface or beneath it — was unparalleled among birds of the Northern Hemisphere. On land, however, they were ludicrous and awkward. The guillemots and murres, cormorants and puffins were not the best of walkers on land, but their movements were considerably quicker and more certain than those of the new arrivals and they seemed to watch the great auk's land movements with ill-concealed amusement.

Actually, the big bird's walk was little more than a grossly exaggerated wobble from side to side. Those muscular legs and feet that were so sure and strong when pushing the sea behind them were suddenly weak and hard put to transport their owners over solid ground.

Far, far to the left they'd lean as the right foot shuffled forward several inches, then equally far to the right as the weight shifted to this foot and the left shuffled forward. Their stubby flipper wings thrashed the air constantly and futilely for a purchase. Frequently they slipped and fell onto the hard rocky surface in a tangle of swinging wings and frantically pumping feet, but always they scrambled up unhurt, cushioned by the thick down of their breasts. Their progress toward the higher portions of the island was for all the world like the extravagantly awkward bumblings of a troupe of circus clowns. Oftentimes when coming downhill they would circumvent disastrous falls by tobogganing on their breasts, pushed along by the feet and guided by the wings.

It was the individual females who now led the way, every one of them followed by one or two jovial males attempting each to walk in her footsteps at the same time. Inevitably they bumped one another, stumbled, rolled and scrambled up again, always vying for that position immediately behind her. The din of thousands of birds calling about them seemed not in the least to affect them, nor did they pay much attention to the scores of birds standing on all sides.

The spaces available for nesting were at a distinct premium. Great jostling crowds of double-crested cormorants had usurped the choice lower cliffside locations overlooking the angry waters. They huddled in dense congregations over incredibly sloppy nests built of decayed seaweed and their own dried excrement scooped into a pile and slightly hollowed out to form a saucer-shaped depression for the two or three or four chalky blue-green eggs. As the great auks shuffled past, these cormorants raised their hooked beaks skyward, inflated their throat sacs and hissed menacingly. The auks paid scant attention and the cormorants very wisely did not press their highly dubious authority.

Nearly every crevice or tiny cranny had its complement of puffin nests. These were hidden deep in the rocky recesses and often the little birds made them even more inaccessible by laboriously excavating loose gravel and larger stones until a tunnel as long as four feet had been formed. To the rear of this cavity a single white egg would be deposited and then guarded with a fierceness belying the diminutive bird's size.

Ever higher the great auks climbed in their search for real estate of their own and they soon had risen above the almost unbelievable masses of murres perched complacently on level ground somewhat inland as well as on the ledges well above the sea. Similar in color and shape to the great auks — though without the distinctive white cheek oval — the murres stood guard over their single sharply pointed greenish eggs splashed with smears of brown and darker green and black and lavender. These eggs lay on the bare rock, very often only inches from the ledge rim and a drop of one hundred feet or more to the water. There was little likelihood of their rolling off, however. So sharply tapered were they that even when a vagrant gust of wind would buffet the ledge and set the eggs rolling, each merely rolled about in the circle of its own radius.

The murres gravely watched the climbing great auks, stretched high on their toes and then began a comically serious bowing and rising, much as guests at a royal party might act upon the approach of the king.

"*Errrr!*" they murmured in many hundreds of voices. "*Errrr! Errrr! Errrr!*"

Gradually the great auks spread widely apart over the heavily populated island until each female found the deserted spot of ground that appealed to her. One stopped with an odd abruptness, turned in a circle several times to her right, back again to the left and then finally squatted on her haunches with a satisfied raspy grunt.

The males stood before her waving their little wings foolishly, almost in circles, serenading her with a series of raucous screeches plainly audible for a mile or more. Faster and faster their wings spun until eventually the pair were thrown off balance to such a degree that they collided and toppled in a heap. Chuckling with something akin to embarrassment, they regained their feet and unconcernedly recommenced the same egregious activity.

The female indicated how deeply impressed she was with all this by nearly falling asleep. She hunched into a deeper squat and permitted her eyelids to half close. This only caused the males to labor harder and screech all the louder to gain her attention and approval . . . and acceptance as mate.

Eventually one of the pair stopped his pinwheeling long enough to take a few deep breaths and apparently to keep from collapsing with nervous prostration. A few feet away he spied a smooth wind-worn pebble. Awkwardly he wobbled over to it and, after falling down twice in the attempt, clumsily managed to pick it up and carry it back to the female. He rasped gratingly and stretched this delightful gift out toward her.

The female bird's eyelids opened briefly, glanced at the bauble and half closed again. She was not to be so easily won. Now the second male spied a rock which was considerably larger, though not quite as smooth. He repeated the actions of the first without falling, but with no greater success than his rival.

Abruptly the throaty murmur of a third male, larger than either of these two, broke in and the sound was somewhat muffled in tone because of a fine silvery herring that was clenched tightly in his beak. This handsome bird was one of the great auks that had re-entered the water immediately after the initial landing. With all the dignity he could muster in view of his preposterous swaying pace and the fish dangling from his mouth, he approached the female and roughly shouldered the other males aside, bowling one of them over in the process.

The female's eyelids opened languidly at his voice but then her gaze sharpened at this new offering. She stared at the newcomer for a long moment, then bowed her head once and straightened from her slouched position. Encouraged, the new suitor wobbled forward another step and stretched his head out.

Carefully avoiding any demonstration of overeagerness, the female casually reached out in a similar manner and plucked the little fish from the male's beak. It disappeared into her mouth and the pair stood frozen in this attitude for the span of almost a minute, their beaks barely touching. Then the tail of the herring reappeared in her beak. With a tiny grunt of acceptance, she bobbed her head again. On the upswing she bit the fish in two, swallowing the head portion and lofting the remainder gently into the air.

Instantly the male snatched it, almost losing his balance as he did so. He then swallowed his share neatly.

Now this larger male turned to face his competitors and his throaty baritone cries rang with unmistakable challenge. Grudgingly, the other two swains clucked and grumbled but fell back as the victor waddled threateningly toward them with his beak poised to thrust like a dagger as soon as he came within range.

Whether it was lack of nerve to face this self-assured challenger or merely comprehension dawning over them as to what had won this female's ultimate acceptance, both males turned and scrambled clumsily to the nearest ledge, where for a long moment they scanned the water far below. Satisfied with its depth and the lack of those deep shadows denoting sub-surface rocks, first one and then the other projected himself into the air. They flashed toward the water like plummeting stones. Only an instant before contact with the water their bodies arched perfectly and they slid beneath the surface with scarcely a splash.

Meanwhile, the victorious male swaggered grandly back to his mate. A year ago he had been in the position of the two vanquished males, but this year he had known what to do. It was an intense moment. From this time forward these two would remain mated. Even should one of them die or be killed, the other would neither accept nor pursue another mate.

The season of summer warmth on Eldey Island is brief and the pair seemed to realize there was no time for extensive coquetries. Waving his flipper wings, the male approached and embraced the female. Their beaks rubbed together for a moment and then the female collapsed and lay still at his feet.

The actual mating act was amazingly brief and, when it was concluded, the pair ambled cliffward side by side, satisfied that their nuptial spot of rock would be claimed by no other great auk. In some indefinable way the site had been marked and would be meticulously avoided by the others of their species. Woe betide the bird of any other species that might trespass on this newly sanctified ground. The steel hardness of a great auk's beak was not to be lightly challenged.

An identical mating act was repeated by the pair each day for six days and during the next two weeks the birds were inseparable. Together they wobbled up the slopes or flashed through the deep greenish gloom of the water near the base of Eldey Island. During the daylight they chased and caught large numbers of fine fat herring fingerlings and capelins in vast schools that literally covered acres of water. During their occasional night hunts, the swift but delectable pilchards — sardines — were caught and devoured by the dozens.

The female was slightly more adept at pursuing and catching the fish than her mate. The male's right wing had once been injured and the outermost pinions had oddly withered and become a dead grayish color. The fish were plentiful, however, and all the great auks were well fed and regained more than the weight lost during the strenuous migration. It was necessary that they become sleek and fat, for when the eggs hatched both parents would have to devote all their time to providing food for just one chick, and would be unable to catch very much for themselves.

Most of the great auks had by now similarly paired off and mated. The only ones that hadn't were a small number of males unsuccessful in their courtship — since there were more males than females — and a handful of birds that had lost mates in previous seasons and would never mate again.

There came a day when the female did not accompany her mate to the ledge and launch herself into the sea in quest of food. Once again she assumed the hunched, languid position she had taken during the early courtship approaches of the males. Her mate continued to fish and eat, occasionally wobbling laboriously to the little patch of rock where the female waited, carrying with him a newly captured small crab or regurgitating a half dozen or more sardines for her. The female accepted the first few offerings but then fell into a deep state of motionlessness which persisted throughout most of the day.

It was late afternoon when she raised her head, opened her brown eyes wide and emitted a piercing shriek. Over the chatter of thousands of birds, the male, swimming a dozen yards from the island far below, heard and identified the call as that of his mate and surged toward shore. He had never climbed the sloping promontory as fast before, but it was still many long minutes before he was able to wobble through the masses of birds and up those relatively steep inclines to the nesting plateau. When he arrived the female was still slouched on her haunches but now her eyes were keenly alive and she chuckled constantly deep in her throat as if highly satisfied with herself.

As the male neared she straightened and stepped back, exposing to view a single huge egg. Creamy white in color, the egg was liberally splotched with irregular streaks of a deep burnt umber and cinnamon, especially toward the larger end. It was almost six inches long and more than half that in diameter, dwarfing the eggs of other sea birds nearby.

That the pair were intensely proud of their egg was apparent in both their actions and their voices. They raised their heads and screeched and chuckled together like a pair of old cronies after hearing some incredibly funny story. Pompously they formed a parade of two and marched round and round the big egg with their queer rolling gait, all the while with their wings turning slowly like little windmills in a gentle breeze.

This pride and concern for their egg was strictly instinctive, but nonetheless impressive. Their actions might have been considerably more dramatic could they have fully realized the significance of this single egg of theirs.

It was undoubtedly the most important egg ever laid by a great auk.

II

I N the beginning there was a darkness without sensation which had no element of time because time meant nothing. Day after day in this darkness the speck of life grew and changed. From a formless, almost liquid mass it took shape and within this shape a minute nucleus of cells commenced a rhythmic contraction and expansion.

There was a continual growth of tissues, an increase in size and a sharper delineation of form. Even though the totality of the darkness persisted, now there came to the little shape the first inklings of physical sensation. There was a vague satisfaction in the usual warmth surrounding it and a stir of keen discomfort against the occasional penetrating chill that came in an alarming wave.

There was movement, too: the stretching of a tiny limb; the arching of a spine still soft but beginning to protest against the cramping caused by the unnatural curvature into which it was forced; the testing swell of *a thousand tiny muscles that had never before tightened.*

For a long period there was a certain comfort in this existence, but soon there came a time when there was only confinement. The pressure of unyielding resistance on all sides was frustrating and the little living shape flexed its miniature muscles and strained ineffectually against this incomprehensible bondage.

Now there came a gradual hardening of tissues as areas of soft cartilaginous material became hard bone and leathery feet and sharp beak. The massive, protuberant eyes saw nothing for there was nothing to see, but still they moved back and forth in their sockets and the eye muscles firmed and strengthened. By degrees there grew in the pulsing nucleus of this fragment of life an irresistible drive to expand and it strained against the walls of its little universe.

The little feet raised and lowered unavailingly in the cramped quarters, seeking a nonexistent purchase. The narrow wings jutting from each side of the organism braced on the smooth firm darkness and strained mightily. The tiny spine arched, relaxed, arched again, moving the oversized head. The beak at the end of this head had grown a hard horny hook at the tip, and there came a time when, as the head moved, the hook rubbed against the confinement and ruptured a thin rubbery membrane. Released from behind this mem-

brane, a pocket of miraculously fresh air flowed all around the tiny organism. A fractional amount was sucked into pinprick nostrils and two pea-sized lungs were inflated for the first time.

Now there came an excitement, a desperation, an incomprehensible but overpowering reaction to the stimulus of air and a need to pierce this darkness and ease the restriction of free movement on all sides.

Again the spine arched . . . and again. The horny hook on the beak rasped gratingly against the walls of the enclosure. The movement was repeated several times, and abruptly there was a sound of splintering, incredibly loud and overwhelmingly exciting within the confines of the shell. The weakened wall split outward in a small hole and the horny beak broke free.

Now the darkness was gone, replaced by a dim formless light that spurred yet greater activity, though it was sensed more than seen. The head moved up and down and from side to side and the splintering increased. The entire beak now plunged through and flakes of the limy walls lay back upon themselves as if hinged and the whole head followed the beak into freedom.

The incredible sweetness of fresh salt air rushed to the tiny lungs and ignited a fire of frenzy in the throbbing little heart. The legs braced and pushed with surprising strength and the little wings flexed. The pressure against four separate places on the interior of the shell by the feet, back and opposing wings was all at once too great to withstand and mammoth fissures spread outward from the break where the head projected.

There was a moment frozen in time when the shell held together as if by miracle only and the elfin bird lurched in a desperate movement to be free of the walls which once encompassed its entire world. The fissures spread wider, held together briefly by more of the tough membrane that coated the interior of the egg.

At length there came a tinkling crash and the shell clove cleanly in half, dumping the weak little organism that had destroyed it onto the hard sun-warmed rock.

The great auk had hatched.

The infant great auk lay still for long moments after its shell had split asunder, utterly exhausted and oblivious to the chuckling murmur booming just above it or to the gentle nudging of a great hard beak nearly as long as the little bird's own body.

Slowly the strength returned to spent muscles, the small body turned upright and its wings braced against the rock beneath it. There was strength enough — but only just enough — to raise the unwieldy head off the ground, to open the beak in a weak protest against the insistent nudging. In that moment when the little great auk's vocal cords formed their very first cry, a mass of soft fleshy material was thrust deeply down its throat and the little bird swallowed convulsively, taking its first meal instinctively and instantly opening its beak and crying for more.

The first few days outside the shell were little more than interrupted feeding times for the baby great auk. The infant's appetite was enormous and no matter how much food was crammed into his mouth and down his throat, as soon as it was swallowed the little beak opened for more and uttered shrill and plaintive cries when its demands were not instantly answered.

One or the other of the parents was always near at hand at first. There was actually little danger from four-legged predators on the small island, but it would have been senseless to leave the newly hatched bird unguarded from the cormorants or gulls — either of which, on occasion, were not above attacking a defenseless nestling and perhaps gouging out an eye or even nipping off a head before irate parents could waddle to the rescue. The great black-backed gull, fully as large as the auks, also watched for nestlings left alone. It would swoop gracefully down, snatch up a little bird in an instant and fly aloft with it, only to open its mouth and drop it to the murderous rocks far below and then dive to its feast. So, for the first few weeks at any rate, the little bird was never left alone.

When the baby great auk had first emerged from the egg it was extremely ugly. As the days progressed, this repulsiveness only intensified until, by the end of the first week, it was wholly hideous to all but its own parents. Shortly after its emergence the horny tip had fallen from the beak, having served its only purpose, leaving behind a perfect miniature of the proud strong beaks of the parent birds. There, however, the resemblance ended.

Unable at first to stand on its own weak legs, the baby bird sprawled grotesquely on his stomach. The hairlike initial egg feathers dried quickly and became a uniform of sparse, bristly gray-black fuzz all over. The head and feet seemed mammothly oversized for the body and the wings were hardly more than bent twigs growing from his sides and helping in some small way to support the lumpy body. He was angular, big-eyed, and squawked demandingly, almost continually, when not being fed. That such an ugly little creature might ever grow up and assume the handsome, stream-lined beauty of his parents appeared inconceivable.

The little great auk's demands on his parents were insistent and unrelenting. During those first two weeks he was aware of little else about him and alternated between three phases — screaming for food, actually gulping it down and lightly napping in the warm sun until more food could be provided.

The speed with which the little bird increased in size was remarkable — though wholly understandable in view of the vast amounts of food he consumed. The two parent birds were kept extremely busy and seldom had time or inclination to catch food for themselves. As a result, while they became leaner the young great auk grew larger and, by the beginning of the fifth week, he was nearing the size of the adult birds and was able to stand and shuffle awkwardly in a weaving, precarious manner that was comically punctuated by frequent flops to the ground. The original egg fuzz was swiftly being replaced by more mature feathers, freckling the gray back with deep glossy black and the equally gray front with emerging whiteness. The difference between fledgling and parent was not so noticeable now. There was even the beginning of the distinctive white spot on his cheek between the beak and the inquisitive brown eye.

With his increased size there came an intensified awareness of his surroundings and a curiosity that must be an ingrained characteristic of all of nature's young creatures. What an exciting place to be hatched! On all sides were birds of various sizes and species, hovering near and tending to the generally unpretty offspring who would one day be replicas of themselves.

Within a dozen feet a gaudily dressed puffin strutted self-importantly back and forth in front of a tunnel scooped out between two adjoining rocks. Though an adult, it was not half the size of the young great auk. So strangely colored was the bird's head that it seemed to be amateurishly hand-painted. The mammoth beak was almost as large as the head and striped with distinct curves of vivid color — yellow, grayish-blue and a deep vermilion. The rim of its mouth was a startlingly brilliant orange and there were grotesque horny bumps and protuberances on the whole beak that would disappear after the breeding season. Like the great auks, its back and wings and crown were a glossy blue-black and its wing undersides and breast a brilliant white. On each side of the head was a large white patch running from the bill almost to the back of the head and nearly round in shape. Slightly above the center of this patch was a large thickly rimmed eye with an unusual pale bluish-white iris.

Occasionally the puffin would strut toward the cliff edge much as the great auks walked but with somewhat more equilibrium. Here it would spring outward and beat its wings violently. It could fly well but seemingly only at great effort and tremendous expenditure of energy. Each time it returned — always by wing — it carried in its mouth one or two or even three fish. That it could manage to retain its hold on the first while catching but not swallowing the one or two others was a tribute to its great skill not only in flying but in underwater swimming. Always as it returned to the burrow with fish in its mouth it voiced that peculiar deep-throated laughter.

The puffin would brook no trespassing on what it considered its private nesting area, which took in a radius of about six feet in all directions from the entrance to the tunnel. Once, when the young great auk's father stumbled and rolled inadvertently onto this territory, the smaller bird attacked savagely and retreated only when the big bird discreetly scrambled out of range of that circle.

Thirty feet below the great auk's rock were the many plateaus and ledges literally teeming with murres, adults and young. The adults stood a foot and a half high and, except for a longer neck, were noticeably similar to the Antarctic penguin. Unlike most of the other sea birds perched directly over the water, those murres on the ledges perched with their backs to the sea. Often, for no apparent reason, they would raise their hoarse baritone voices in unison and almost drown out the sound of the thundering surf below them with their loud *"Errrr! Errrr errrr! Errrr!"*

Throughout the day the murres would throw themselves from the ledges with almost reckless abandon, stop the plummeting fall with rapidly beating wings before hitting the sea, make a wide circle in the air and then return to alight on their previous launching spot. There seemed to be no sense in the maneuver but the birds apparently enjoyed it tremendously and appeared inordinately proud of their feat when they returned. Occasionally they would slice into the water below with a moderate splash, bob high on the surface for a few moments and then dive in search of small herrings and capelin.

Scattered here and there within view on level rock ledges and flat plainlike areas not populated by the murres or guillemots were the occasional dull brown skuas. Four or five inches larger than the murres, they closely resembled sea gulls except for their larger size. With great intensity they would watch the fishing activities of the Iceland gull or dovekie, the murres and guillemots or Arctic terns. When any of the latter caught a nice fish too big to be swallowed in flight by neatly tossing it back in the throat, these thieves would attack with great ferocity until the other bird was forced to drop its prey with an angry shriek, at which moment the attack would end and the brown robber would swiftly dive and snatch the lost morsel out of the air before it could hit the water. Whenever one of these pirates would glide overhead, the little great auk's parents would crouch and glare, rumbling deep warnings for the bird to keep its distance.

By the end of the fifth week the little great auk was wobbling here and there in the area surrounding his home grounds. With imprudent curiosity he would lower his head to take a closer look at the fledgling murres or dovekies or cormorants and more than once was painfully nipped as a warning to keep a respectful distance. More and more he seemed drawn to the sea and spent long hours standing on the very brink of a frightful drop to the water.

From this vantage point the coastline of Iceland and the many smaller islands scattered out from its shores were clearly visible to his sharp eyes. One small island only two miles to the south was particularly interesting because of the bustling activity about it. Considerably smaller than Eldey Island, it neither towered so high nor were its seaward approaches so severe. Immense flocks of sea birds — particularly murres — nested here. Their numbers were so great that even standing room over the whole island was at a premium.

Often this view was impaired by the frequent heavy fogs so common in the early morning hours off southwestern Iceland. It was on just such a morning that a strange and troubling drama unfolded before the young bird's uncomprehending eyes.

Only a short time before the fog began lifting, unusual sounds wafted toward Eldey Island from the direction of the smaller island. There was a grinding clank and a deep splash, followed by other, regularly spaced splashes and strange murmurings like no other sounds the little great auk had ever before heard. The source of these sounds became visible as the fog lifted.

A quarter mile off the little island floated a large sailing ship at anchor. Three dinghies were just effecting an easy landing on the near rock-scattered shore. From each of these boats alighted six or seven men armed with short stout clubs. They made the boats fast, and swiftly laid down long planks leading from the gunwales to the shore.

A thunderous chorus of *"Errrr! Errrr!"* rose clearly into the air from the little island as a number of men spread out and encircled a nearby cluster of a hundred or more murres. Slowly but relentlessly the men drove the birds before them toward the boats. Pressed by the masses behind them, the lead birds waddled down the shore and then onto the planks. Each boat had two planks leading to it and each plank was tended by a club wielder in the boat. As the birds reached the end of the plank over the open boat, they were struck by short vicious blows on the head and their carcasses sprawled into the boats. On they came, dumbly following the bird before them and suffering the same fate. Even at this distance the keen ears of the little great auk could hear the chilling thumps of clubs striking the birds.

The Eldey Island bird population remained remarkably quiet, though visibly nervous, and watched the slaughter continue for more than two hours. When the boats were filled to capacity with birds, the men walked farther inland and swung their clubs at the birds waddling awkwardly before them and unable to outpace their attackers. Twice the dinghies put to sea and delivered their cargo to the parent ship before enough of the murres became alarmed and flew or swam off the island to make a further onslaught unprofitable.

The carnage was fantastic. Many hundreds of birds had been slain. Other hundreds of young birds, incapable of fending for themselves, would die of starvation or exposure when the parent birds did not return. The mournful cries of the birds from this little island continued throughout the day, long after the boats had been gobbled up by the large ship and the ship itself had been lost to sight toward Iceland's Cape Reykjanes in the south. Even after the fall of darkness, the little great auk awoke occasionally to the lingering cries of anguish and injury still sounding from the island.

By the next morning the birds of Eldey Island had resumed their normal garrulity and had apparently forgotten the chilling sights and sounds of the previous day. Life went on for them exactly as it had the day before the incident. Some of the birds here had seen such sights before and a few others had actually been survivors of similar tragedies.

Toward the end of the second month, the young great auk was guided to lower levels on the island by his parents and here he encountered other young auks practically identical to himself, though few were as large. All now had their full feathering and most were larger and healthier appearing than the adult birds. There was considerable hoarse croaking and shrill squealing as the great auks mingled, and a feeling of excitement filled the younger birds. Today they would enter the sea for the first time, leaving behind their bumbling awkwardness of land travel and learning the swift grace of their kind in the water.

The young great auk was one of the first to be nudged toward the water by his parents, who flanked him and muttered meaningfully as they directed him toward the sloping rock. Carefully he waddled downward between them and then a wave slapped up and spread across his lower legs and tail, nearly knocking him down. A wild thrill charged through him with this first contact with the sea. At the peak of this wave the large male flopped out into the water and bobbed away with it like a cork as it receded. He stopped a dozen feet away and rasped for the youngster to follow.

Before the young great auk had an opportunity to do so of his own volition, the decision was taken away from him. Just as another wave swirled up around his ankles, he was bowled over from behind by another youngster like himself who had lost his balance on the sloping rock. Together they flopped into the water with legs and wings churning wildly and then, amazingly, they were floating neatly near the male bird.

Croaking happily, they kicked their feet and found themselves swimming easily, surging up and over the swells as if they had done this all their lives. The female and the parents of the other bird joined the trio in the water. There were delighted chucklings and a generally good-natured thrashing of the water by all concerned.

Quite suddenly the four adult birds disappeared beneath the surface and a moment of panic gripped the two youngsters. The mother of the other bird surfaced lightly, barked a short command and disappeared again. The youngster paddled about in confusion and then headed for the sloping rock where more of the young great auks were being led into the water. There was a frantic shriek as the adult grabbed his foot and pulled him under the surface. At the same moment the young great auk felt his own foot gripped firmly but not painfully and, despite the thrashing of his wings, he was drawn downward.

Grayish withered feathers on the right wingtip indicated it was his father who had pulled him under. They were now a dozen feet below the surface and the water was almost as clear to his eyes as the air. Far below he spied the other two adults swimming slowly, followed by their youngster. His own mother was off to his right and, as the grip on his leg was released, he surged toward her.

He was swimming! Smoothly, without undue effort, he glided through the water with the skill of a fish and with a grace and economy of motion he'd never before experienced. It was exhilarating, and he followed the two adult birds past looming submerged rocks and great jagged shelves.

They didn't stay under water very long on this first attempt — not more than a minute — but it was the most glorious experience the young bird had ever known. He croaked exultantly as they surfaced and instantly submerged again. In this weightless world of water he had found his kingdom.

The remainder of that day and in the weeks which followed, he spent most of his time in the water. Although instinctively an excellent swimmer, he still had much to learn in order to become as adept at this game as his parents. This he learned quickly enough with his first attempts to catch a fish.

The three of them were perhaps five fathoms beneath the surface when far ahead they spied a huge school of herring fingerlings. Instantly the adults shot ahead, far outdistancing the youngster. Expertly they circled the school, causing it to bunch together in a tight mass. First the female, then the male shot into this cluster, each emerging with a silvery herring perhaps five inches in length. Without pause they continued to herd the school, circling round and round them. They quickly swallowed their catches and now repeated the attack with the same results.

The young great auk overtook them and without hesitation plunged into the mass of greenish-backed silvery fish. There were so many bunched together he couldn't possibly miss . . . but he did. His beak opened and closed with repeated snaps, but it closed on nothing but water. The startled fish broke ranks and scattered in darting clusters and the three birds sped to the surface for more air.

It was some time before the young one learned the wisdom of carefully herding the schooled fishes in the

manner exhibited by his parents. It was even longer
before he learned not to plunge wildly at the school
in general but to select one individual fish as his target
and never let his attention be diverted from that
single fish.

The subsurface swimming of the great auks was
a delight to behold. Both wings and feet were used for
locomotion and maneuvering. With great speed the
wings beat alternately through the water in perfect
cadence with the strong pushing of the splayed web-
feet, propelling the bird with extraordinary velocity.
Few were the fish that could outswim or outmaneuver
a wily and experienced great auk. The birds could
swim, turn, even reverse direction with incredible
speed and agility and any small fish that ventured very
far away from the protection of rocks and crevices
was in grave danger indeed if the great auk
chanced by.

Often these great auks descended well over two
hundred feet deep in their search for food fish or, if
conditions necessitated it, in order to escape danger.
They could swim under water for nearly half a mile
before their need for air would force them to resurface. While they normally stayed under the surface
for less than six minutes, in a pinch they could remain
below for as long as eleven minutes!

The sport which soon became the delight of the

young great auk was seeking out, chasing and catching the various species of fish in these waters which not always ran in schools. Many of these fish — the slim, young gray pollacks, for example — would, when they couldn't escape into their rocky crevices, perform the most amazing types of gyrations in their frantic attempts to get away. Many of them did escape the young bird at first, but as he learned to estimate distances, to flash in and out of the rocks and never to vary his attention from the single fish selected for pursuit, regardless of how many fish swam between him and his prey or how close they came, he rarely missed snapping the fish up in his beak.

At about the same time he also learned the folly of overestimating his own prowess. This came about when he pursued and overtook quite a large codfish. The fish was nearly twice his own length and easily four times heavier than he. After chasing it for several hundred yards along the dim bottom nearly fifteen fathoms down, he finally managed to grip it tightly in his beak just in front of the tail.

The terrified fish thrashed about in a frenzy to be free and the whipping of its powerful tail nearly broke the young bird's neck. After being dragged along for a full forty yards, the young great auk conceded defeat, disengaged his hold and painfully beat his way back to the surface. The remainder of his day was spent in dejected solitude, hunched on a deserted rocky prominence jutting from the surface near the island's base.

By the next morning the young great auk had apparently forgotten his humiliating encounter of the previous day. He played carelessly in the water with other young great auks and joined in the pleasurable games of herding vast schools of herring and pilchard, menhaden and capelin as cowboys might herd cattle — occasionally darting in to snap up a particularly appealing fish but mostly savoring the keen enjoyment of the hunt. In the process he was learning one of the basic techniques of survival for his species.

A strange thing resulted, however. Although the young great auk encountered many codfish near Eldey Island, and codfish were eaten voraciously by the other great auks, after his initial encounter with that large one he never pursued another.

III

BY THE beginning of August only traces of the first
fuzz feathers remained here and there in the
young great auk's new adult plumage. All vestiges
of his initial ugliness had disappeared and he was a
truly handsome bird. His body was thick and strong,
yet built in lines which permitted him to bullet
through the water in a blur of speed, outpacing all his
companions and even a number of the adults.

The original eighty great auks had swelled their
ranks during this breeding season by twenty-eight.
More or less gregarious in their habits, the flock stayed
reasonably close together and often an armada of
the black-and-white birds ventured off en masse on
hunting trips. At such times an interesting phenom-
enon would occur.

The leaders, wily birds with many seasons to their
credit, would surge ahead seeking out the great schools
of food fish. Time would not be wasted on those
schools where there was not enough to feed the entire

flock many times over. Sometimes the fish were found by following the movements of the flying sea birds who could spot the schools at great distances from above and arrow to the attack in screaming dives. Just as often, however, the great auk leaders would submerge and wing through the twilight world of a hundred feet or more below the surface, ever on the alert for that massive smokelike cloud which signified a large school.

Unlike the other sea birds when such a school was located, the great auks did not immediately slash to the attack. Over one hundred birds were in the flock and if such direct onslaught were initiated only the relatively few in the van would be able to make any significant catches before the school would disperse to hide in the shadowy pockets along rocky bottoms.

Immediately upon spying such a shoal of fish, the leaders would surface and fling a grinding call back at the main body of the flock. The birds would accelerate until the water behind them was churned white with the foam of their passage. Upon catching up to the leaders, they would mill about for a moment and then the entire raft of them would slip beneath the surface, leaving behind a calm and apparently deserted ocean.

It was on a darkly overcast day that the young great auk participated in his first of these exciting hunts. The quarry having been located, the flock spread out under water in a great cup shape; the leading birds, forming the rim of the "cup," encircled the schooled fish without attacking, while those following as the body of the cup forced the fish to bunch together into an incredibly dense mass. Occasionally here and there a small flurry of activity broke out when a segment of the fish attempted to break free of the ranks. Like shepherd dogs herding their sheep, however, the nearest great auks cut them off and adroitly forced them back into the mass.

Gradually, carefully, avoiding threatening movements which might panic the school, the birds headed them out toward deeper water away from the shelving rocks where they might escape when the eventual attack was launched. The deeper the water became, the closer to the surface the schooled fish were forced.

The other sea birds on nearby islands were well aware of the significance of the flock's impressive disappearance under water. Immediately the air became filled with wildly screaming birds creating a cacophony audible for miles in all directions and attracting ever more birds. The great black-backed gulls and smaller white Iceland gulls sailed gracefully to the spot, followed by delicate kittiwakes and the coarser skuas and green and double-crested cormorants. Jaegers, storm petrels and the Arctic terns wheeled and flapped expectantly high over the water, while closer to the surface in vociferous anticipation flew the black guillemots, puffins and dovekies, the razor-billed auks and murres, all with wildly straining wings. Circling the fringes of the strangely mixed assemblage were large northern gannets and Manx shearwaters and fulmars. The air was turbulent with darting birds and rang with the intermingling of a thousand different bird voices.

Meanwhile the great auks tightened their ranks, forcing the fish even closer together and causing them to rise more steeply to the surface. A great fear spread through the schooled fish now as the shadows of many hundreds of birds darkened the water above, and in their panic they did the worst possible thing. Voluntarily streaking toward the surface now, they threw themselves out of the water in frantic attempts to skip away from the danger like flat stones skipped across still water. More than two acres of the water surface erupted as untold millions of six-inch capelins broke and lofted inches through the air, falling back only to jump again instantly. The din was fantastic and sounded like a great hailstorm beating the water.

Into the water arrowed the dovekies and puffins, the guillemots and murres and razor-billed auks. Under water they swam into and through the very midst of the thick school, snatching and swallowing capelins with greedy rapidity. The big northern gannets flew in with long sweeping curves several dozen feet above the water surface, terminated by a steep diagonal dive into the thickest portions of the schooled fish. A single dive would produce for each gannet three or six or even a dozen fish before it surfaced and took off in another great curving flight to repeat the action.

The cormorants plunged to the surface, bobbed for an instant and then dived into the melee, catching their fish under water in great numbers. Perhaps most graceful were the gulls, terns and kittiwakes, who, as the fish leaped from the water, would wing close to the surface and pluck them out of the air. Often, as these birds climbed higher to swallow their catch, they were forced to drop it by the attacks of marauding jaegers and skuas who themselves caught the falling fish and gobbled them down.

The fulmars and shearwaters thrashed about on the surface, catching occasional live fish and snatching up the bits and pieces of fish severed and dropped by other birds. Through it all, wings flapping gently, the storm petrels ran delicately across the water surface, here and there darting to grab a small capelin.

As the instigators of this vast feast, the great auks remained unperturbed by the frenzied activity their efforts had caused. In and out of the milling silvery clouds of fish they flashed, each time swallowing one or two or three fish. Even the most inexperienced of the young birds was soon filled to capacity.

The young great auk had swallowed seventeen of the capelins and was so full that the last one's tail still projected from the corner of his beak, despite repeated swallowings. The herding action of the great auks gradually diminished and the schooled fish began to scatter. The feeding birds on and below the surface spread over an ever-widening area and within a few moments the activity was over. Though virtually every bird of each of the species had fed to capacity, the dent made in the capelin population of this one school was infinitesimal.

Most of the birds swam or flew leisurely back to their islands to sit in lazy contemplation of the heavy clouds as their meals digested. Near the ocean floor the capelins regrouped and skimmed back toward shallower water and the comparative safety of the rocky ledges. They swam casually, their horrible encounter already forgotten.

The great auks now scattered somewhat, with various clusters heading back toward Eldey Island and others merely riding the large swells with evident enjoyment. Here and there little groups of six or eight splashed the water playfully and grumbled good-naturedly to one another.

The young great auk was very content and highly

pleased with his own performance in the hunt. Only twice had he failed to snap up the fish he had singled out and both times it was due to the interference of another bird. Once a little puffin darted past and snatched up his quarry only an instant before his own beak closed where it had been. The other time, nearer the surface, a huge gannet had slashed into the water, nearly colliding with him and making him veer sharply, thus losing track of his fish.

Now, drifting aimlessly on the rather choppy surface and sometimes spinning in a complete circle with the erratic backwash of a wave trough, he spied far ahead of him a group of about thirty great auks, most of which were young birds. Immediately curious, he headed toward them — but the gap closed with surprising slowness, as the distant group was swimming determinedly toward the southwest and had nearly a two-mile headstart on him.

The young great auk had become, in these months, one of the largest of the young; and since most of the youngsters were by now considerably heavier than their own parents, he was consequently one of the biggest birds of the flock. While his proficiency in swimming and diving may not yet have equaled that of the older birds, he was nonetheless a powerful swimmer and he put extra power into his strokes now to overtake the group ahead.

In a short time, Eldey Island, despite its height and the young great auk's keen vision, was nearly out of sight behind and the Iceland coast was no longer visible. Even Eldey was only a dark little smudge on the horizon which became momentarily visible when the bird was raised high on the crest of heavy swells which were now rapidly evolving into huge waves.

For the first time the young bird paid particular attention to the sky. The overcast had considerably darkened and he could smell the approaching storm in the air. Low on the southwestern horizon ahead of him a band of angry yellowish and slate-gray clouds swept toward him and it became increasingly difficult to swim against the white-capped waves.

The young great auk had experienced storms before. Several times during the past month, before he'd even learned to swim, the island had been lashed by brief storms which had caused him to lie face down between the bulk of his parents' protecting bodies to keep from being blown against the rocks or off the ledges by the savage gusts. The rain had not bothered him and had, in fact, been a strange and rather delightful surprise. Who would have thought water in such quantity could have been seen this far above the sea?

Now, still a quarter mile behind the bobbing birds

he was following, the first stirrings of fear came to him. This storm was not quite the same as those he'd already been through. The clouds were more ominous and the wind had sprung up so swiftly that surface swimming now became a matter of pumping laboriously to the crest of a wave and then bursting up, over and down into the deep trough on the opposite side. He felt suddenly very weak, very insignificant and impotent.

The darkness increased and the wind hissing over the cresting waves picked up the salt water and carried it parallel to the raging surface in fearfully stinging droplets. The flock ahead was no longer visible as a group. Here and there as he topped a crest the young great auk could see scattered individuals, but only a few at a time. Some had turned and were swimming back toward him, while others continued to buck the buffeting water.

With a tremendous howling the gale burst over the bird, actually picking him off a wave crest and tumbling him a dozen yards back in the direction from which he'd come. Terrified now, the young great auk submerged and swam desperately back toward the island. He could not stay under water for very long, however. The exertion already expended in overtaking the others, combined with the heavy weight of fish inside his stomach, slowed him, sapped his strength.

He surfaced within one hundred yards of where he had dived. Nothing was visible now in the roaring gloom except raw angry waves smashing him with brutal force, tumbling him over and over and choking him in briny foam.

Again he dived but it was a shorter dive than before as it had been difficult to take a full breath without choking on the water slashed against him. He resurfaced and pumped furiously with wings and feet, gaining the crest of a tremendous wave. It carried him momentarily like a surfboarder and enabled him to suck in a deep breath. As he crashed down into the trough of the waves again, he dived down and down. Forty feet below the whipping surface he leveled off, paused briefly to vomit the remaining undigested fish in his stomach and then swam instinctively back toward the island with strong sure strokes.

It was calm, deceptively peaceful this far below and he would have stayed down longer, but it became necessary to resurface. Still the island was not in sight. The gale slashed at him and the waves hammered him with heavy blows which bowled him over and filled his nostrils and throat with water so he couldn't breathe. The brutal beating he was taking swept the strength from his muscles as easily as the merciless wind swept the salt spray from the waves.

The young great auk's eyes closed and for a

moment he rolled willy-nilly with the waves. Then he righted himself, caught a breath and dived again. He was down only a dozen feet when his need for air became imperative and he had to return to the surface, to the brunt of that deadly lashing maelstrom.

There comes a point where even though the limbs continue to struggle automatically, the mind becomes numbed, stunned. So it happened with the young great auk. With strangely methodical movements his legs and wings continued to pump. Sometimes he was on the surface, sometimes cascaded below it in a welter of foam. Once he roused enough to realize instinctively he was pumping in the wrong direction, but it didn't really make any difference, for he could have made no headway. Another time a wave carried him on his back, head submerged, while his legs and wings still thrust, thrust like a machine someone has forgotten to switch off.

He couldn't know how long this automatic, almost senseless swimming continued, but he was unexpectedly struck a smashing blow which numbed one wing and served to jar him from his trance. The blow was too rough, too solid and hurt too much to have been a wave. He raised his head and his eyes focused, seeing, for just an instant before he was smashed against it again, the sheer face of towering rock which could only be an island, perhaps even Eldey Island.

Hurt, stiff, barely able to move, the young bird scanned the rock for a ledge, a ramp up which he might flounder away from this devastating battering, but he saw none. Again he was slammed against the rock, and once more. Dazedly he felt himself sucked down into a deep trough and then lifted high, high and literally thrown at the cliff. His tired muscles tensed for the expected massive blow from which he could not hope to recover, but it didn't come. Instead he felt the flat surface of a rock sliding beneath him as he was thrust up and out of the sea onto a smooth plateau. Tenpin-like he tumbled and spun with the cascading water and then dropped off the leeward side of the flat rock surface into a small hollow. Braced closely by rock on three sides, the dazed bird simply crouched as the wind shrieked through narrow crevices and intermittent deluges of water burst over him and nearly filled his hollow, only to drain rapidly away with the recession of the wave.

It seemed the storm would never end, though some time after the deeper darkness of nightfall blotted out all vision its fury eased off somewhat, and the pounding waves no longer tumbled over the high ledge into the hollow with such frequency.

Toward morning the wind abated with almost frightening suddenness, and though the sea continued an unnatural heaving and pounding, and the daylight when it came was a slow, dismal graying, a certain quieting returned to the atmosphere.

The young great auk looked dead. His normally slick and well-preened feathers were watersoaked and bedraggled. Had it not been for the rocks against which he was braced, he would certainly have collapsed, for his head was sunk low on the disheveled breast and one foot was planted atop the other in an unusual and unnatural attitude.

For an interminable period the bird did not move. The minutes crept into hours and the hours into half a day before the eyes blinked with returning awareness. Even then it was many minutes before he moved, and the movement, when attempted, was slow and engendered excruciating pain. First a slight shudder ran through him and the trembling shook free those droplets of water still clinging to the soggy plumage. Then he slid the one foot off the other and the toes of both feet clenched downward for a better grip on the rough rock. He slowly, painfully raised his head and let it couch tiredly erect in the hollow of his shoulders. Thus he stood without moving more for another full hour.

At length he turned his head and looked about. He could see nothing but rock and gray sky. His beak opened slightly and a miserable little grunt issued from it. It seemed to startle him and he repeated it, louder this time and with almost a touch of amazement at discovering that he was a live bird who could cause such a sound.

He stretched his wings slowly and the left one hurt terribly. He could still move it but the muscles were severely wrenched and felt torn nearly out of place. Again he shook himself and then performed an act which proved him on the road to recovery: with great care and deliberation he began preening himself, sliding the rumpled feathers between his beak, squeezing out any accumulation of water, straightening the disarrayed spines of each and nudging them carefully back into place.

Now a colossal hunger assailed him and he found that destructive though the storm had been, it had helped him in one respect. Lying on its back a few feet away, broken but still fresh, was the carcass of a small spiny lobster. Painfully the young great auk shuffled over to it and plunged his beak through a break in the horny greenish shell. He gulped several mouthfuls of the viscera in rapid succession, cleaning out the body cavity expertly. The tail meat was next, coming free with the probing of his beak in one large curved strip like a white finger. It disappeared quickly. Finally the heavy claws were crushed in the strong beak and the meat neatly extracted and devoured. All the bird left behind was the hollow chitinous husk of the crustacean.

It was remarkable how swiftly this bit of food reacted in him. Almost visibly there was a return of strength to his limbs and his gaze sharpened. Less than fifteen minutes later the young great auk waddled purposefully out of his three-sided rock pen without a glance at the remains of the lobster.

The bird found himself on the uppermost reaches of a tiny pentagonal rock islet less than two dozen yards across. To the east, bleakly silhouetted between the angry gray water and the still dark gray sky, were the distant craggy bluffs of Iceland. A quarter turn to the right and the young bird saw the welcome pinnacles of his own Eldey Island only a mile distant, its usual morning beacon fires reduced to ashes in this wan light.

Without hesitation the bird shuffled to a ledge ten feet above the swirling waters and plunged in. There was much pain in swimming at first, for his muscles had taken great punishment. It was well that he swam, however, for without this exercise of the strained tissues they would quickly have stiffened until even the slightest movement would have been agony.

By the time he neared the island he was much improved. The muscles that had begun to knot had now loosened and his swimming was almost normal, although this short distance had greatly tired him and he rested numerous times during the crossing. He found himself on the opposite side of the island to that launching spot with which he was most familiar and he swam slowly but steadily around the perimeter of rocks to that point.

Here and there in low pockets of the rocks were the mangled bodies of birds. A large number of murres had apparently died and there were guillemots and gannets as well. Occasionally the little gray-blue body of an Arctic tern or a white Iceland gull drifted aimlessly upside down in an eddy between half submerged rocks. At one point he passed a shallow V-shaped crevice ending a dozen feet back in the rock and at least six dead puffins lay stacked together, their bodies jammed tightly into the farthest recesses of the crevice.

At length the young bird let a swell carry him onto the sloping rock and wearily waddled ashore. It took him a long time to make his way to that level rocky platform where he was hatched. In the growing dusk he was reunited with the two adult great auks who were standing disconsolately at the spot.

The adults muttered deeply at his approach and for a short time filled the air with a peculiar moaning cry. They rubbed their strong beaks gently across his and caressed his shoulders and wings. Although bigger than either of them now, the young great auk stood gratefully between them and slouched comfortably into the remembered safety of their nearness.

He slept very deeply that night.

Early the next morning Eldey Island displayed to the sea and distant Iceland its beacon of fire red. A brisk cool breeze had swept away the dirty gray clouds and the sky was extraordinarily clear and clean with almost limitless visibility.

It was soon apparent that the storm had wreaked havoc on the sea bird population. Some of the flying species — the black-backed gulls, the gannets, the shearwaters and fulmars seemed to have vanished altogether. The murre population was reduced and few puffins and dovekies were in view. Almost all the species — with the exception of the cormorants, which seemed as numerous as ever — had suffered heavy losses.

There was a subdued, grieving atmosphere blanketing the island. Some of the flyers — the Arctic terns and storm petrels, a few gannets and shearwaters — returned after several days, but not in the numbers originally there.

Of all the species, none had suffered so greatly as the great auks. Before the storm came there had been over one hundred of them scattered about the island. Now there remained only seventy-one. Bad enough of itself, the tragedy was even worse than numbers alone could show, compounded by the fact that of the twenty-eight great auks hatched here in early June, only five remained alive. The young great auk was the only survivor of the group that had been swimming toward the southwest when the storm struck. The eleven adult birds and nineteen other juveniles in that group were never seen again. Four youngsters were lost near the island, as were two adults. Another badly battered adult female who managed to return to the island at the height of the storm was so critically injured that for two days she sat hunched miserably beside a great boulder and on the third morning she was dead.

Nature is a cruel teacher but she has kindly endowed many of her creatures with an inability to dwell on the horrors of the past. For a few days the birds of Eldey Island cast suspicious glances now and again at the sea and sky as if expecting a re-enactment of what had occurred. When it did not happen, they merely forgot about it and resumed their normal lives in the cheerless North Atlantic. There was more than enough to occupy them with the simple day-to-day requirements of survival.

The great schools of fish which had been so numerous in these waters all through the early summer months now became noticeably scarce. A full day's hunt for the great auks seldom resulted, as it once did, in all the bellies being filled with rich food. Now, if the pangs of hunger were to be stilled, it became necessary to snatch up even the tiny crabs and bitter little rockfish that had heretofore been ignored when the easier-to-catch schooled fish were in abundance. The flock was required to travel farther and farther for less and less food.

Once in a while, to be sure, a school of menhaden or sardines were encountered, resulting in a frenzied orgy of feeding, but it happened too rarely. The fish were moving away as the frigid bite of the North Atlantic intensified. Each day small groups of flying birds would spring from their ledges by twos and threes, wheel about in aimless circles until the flock became of substantial size and then, with grating screeches hurled behind them, they would disappear toward the east or west.

Disturbingly strange marine creatures were seen now, swimming near the surface where the water was still slightly warmed by a hesitant sun. There cruised the deep blue shadows of three huge mackerel sharks and there, over toward the coastline, a large herd of porpoises frisked out of the water in a series of spectacular jumps before disappearing southward. Not unfamiliar to the great auks in these waters, the porpoises merely seemed to be in much larger groups now.

The young great auk had a severe fright one day when the gigantic sixty-foot bulks of two right whales surfaced, one on each side of him, and blew out a stinking spray of moist exhalation. They were no more than twenty yards apart. He dived instantly and was even more terror-stricken at their size under water. These behemoths, however, paid no attention to him and, after that initial encounter, he paid little attention to them.

One day toward the close of August, the young great auk was engaged in the usual daily search for food with another youngster and five adults, including his parents. Suddenly his father beat the water frantically with his wings and screeched terribly. He and two of the other adults, a male and a female, now began a weird surface-thrashing swim away from the group. The two remaining adults — his mother and another female — grated a hoarse command and dived. He and the other youngster followed instantly. Although both were larger than the females, it was all they could do to keep up with the adults' headlong swim under the water to the island a few hundred yards away. Unhesitatingly the females thrust themselves up the sloping rock and scrambled out of the water, the youngsters immediately behind them.

His mother stood facing the sea and emitted a piercing screech which was echoed by the other female. Several small rafts of great auks within hearing looked up sharply at the sound and instantly submerged. A large flock of razor-billed auks resting on the surface thundered along the top of the water and took off laboriously.

Out near where they had been swimming, the young great auk saw a flash of black and white that was far too large to be one of the three adults. Then there was another. Three more angled in from another direction. They were huge shapes and as one maneuvered in a tight turn near the surface, the young great auk could see it looked like a large piebald porpoise perhaps twenty-five feet in length. More of these big animals moved in until there were over fifteen.

The sloped landing rock was now erupting with great auks scurrying in almost comical haste to be out of the water. One of the great auks was the female that had splashed off with the young great auk's father and the other male in an attempt to divert the attention of the monsters while the youngsters reached safety. The diversion worked, but it was costly. The two males did not reappear.

The predators were a herd of killer whales, those

frightful terrors of the sea which fear nothing and will attack anything that swims, regardless of whether it is a little flock of sea birds or the blue whale, largest animal in the world. Their gluttony is unparalleled; one such killer was harpooned by mariners and found to contain fourteen seals and thirteen porpoises, all swallowed whole.

Singly, the killers were fast and thoroughly dangerous, although an individual killer would have been hard put to maneuver well enough to chase and catch a fleeing great auk. But these beasts were seldom encountered alone and when they attacked in a pack, as they just had, it was virtually impossible to outmaneuver one without swimming directly into the path of two or three others.

Hungry though they were, the great auks remained out of the water the rest of that day. The next morning they resumed their normal feeding and fishing activities as if nothing had happened.

When the young great auk entered the water, his keen glance noted and then dismissed as inconsequential the tips of several broken pinion feathers bobbing in a little pocket between the rocks. Had he inspected them closely, he would have noted an unusual thing about them.

The feathers were an unnatural grayish color and strangely withered at the ends, as from an old injury.

IV

IT WAS a strange paradox that the great auks, last of the migrating birds to reach Eldey Island in the spring, were the first to begin their fall migration. Other birds on the islands had begun to form into squads and platoons and companies, wheeling and circling in the air around the island and always calling others to join them, but they eventually settled back to their perches or resumed their fishing. These dry runs were in the nature of rehearsals for the day when they would lift and circle but not return, instead striking out toward the coastlines of Europe or North America to follow them southward to warmer climes.

The champions of these migratory flights were the Arctic terns, beginning their marathon southern flight shortly after the great auks swam away. The island areas off the coasts of Iceland and Greenland were close to the southern limit of their breeding haunts and often they nested as far north as seven or eight degrees from the North Pole, where the adults often had to scoop out the snow that had accumulated in their nests. Very late in August these terns began dipping and wheeling, moving always southward and picking up ever greater numbers of their fellows as they progressed. By the time the flocks from the northernmost portions of the globe had reached Iceland early in September, their numbers had swelled to the tens of thousands which darkened the ocean sky and which appeared from a distance to be a great black cloud of smoke stringing out beyond the range of vision along the horizon.

In just twenty-two weeks, this elegant little bird, clad in his pale bluish-gray with a distinctive crown of lustrous green-black, would travel over twenty-two thousand miles — wintering deep in the Antarctic for a relatively short while before beginning the strenuous flight back to the Arctic Circle. Because of this extensive migration, the Arctic tern has more hours of daylight than any other animal on earth. The midnight sun of the far north has already risen before the terns arrive at their breeding grounds and it never sets during their stay. By the same token, the birds never see a sunset during the first seven or eight weeks of their stay in the Antarctic and for the remainder of the time the sun slides only a little way below the horizon and darkness never falls. The Arctic terns, therefore, enjoy full daylight for at least eight months out of the year, and the remaining four months — as they migrate northward and southward — have considerably more daylight than darkness.

Most of the other flyers in that Icelandic sea did not begin their migrations for several weeks after the great auks swam off. Although the vast schools of food fish were moving southward, there was still an ample supply for many of these birds. As a result, the migrations of a number of these species were remarkably short in distance.

The great auk's hardy cousin, the razor-billed auk, for example, usually wintered in the coastal areas of New Brunswick, seemingly not in the least discomfited by the bitter winter blasts which lashed it. Occasionally a small flock would extend their journey and winter as far south as North Carolina, but this was very rare.

The big skuas and fulmars wintered in Newfoundland and Nova Scotia and the vast flocks of murres alternately swam and flew the relatively short distance to the rugged Maine coast for their winter vacation. The black guillemots and puffins took up quarters that were seldom south of Cape Cod, while the dovekies flew on to the shores of Long Island.

Once in a while, depending on how severe the winter became, the great black-backed gull flew all the way down to Florida instead of his normal stopping place of Delaware. The jaegers glided into New Jersey.

Of the flying birds, only five — the Arctic terns, cormorants, northern gannets, storm petrels and shearwaters — made extensive migrational flights. From the North Atlantic the big shearwaters drifted down the coastlines of four continents: Europe and Africa to the east, spending the winter off the Cape of Good Hope; North and South America to the west, wintering off Chile's Cape Horn. The gannets migrated to the Gulf of Mexico and North Africa, Madeira and the Canary Islands. Storm petrels winged to the sunny Mediterranean and Africa. Many of the double-crested and green cormorants flew only as far as North Carolina, but large numbers often continued down to the Gulf of Mexico.

All of these birds had a tremendous advantage over the great auks in their ability to fly. Not only was flight faster for them, when they tired they could swoop to the water to rest or even to continue their migration by swimming for a distance. Not the great auks.

Never before having experienced a migration, the young great auk could not identify this great excitement which gripped and changed the flock. He felt it, too, and the very fact that he didn't know its cause excited him all the more. Each passing day there was a great urge, an almost uncontainable desire to thrust out from the island and begin swimming away without a backward glance. The strange tremulous gratings almost constantly bubbling from the beaks of the adult great auks only served to increase the strange obsession, and for hours on end he would perch on shore or float gracefully on rolling swells of the sea, looking first to the north and then to the west.

There was an increased desire for companionship in him and the others now. Seldom did the individual birds or even small clusters move away on their own to fish or frolic. They moved in one great body which, but for the devastating storm that had punished them so terribly, would have been considerably larger. They fished and swam together and there was an odd, almost unconscious jockeying for position as the flock swam. Several old males and females were always in the van and one of these, a tremendous old male of ten years or more — the same one, in fact, that had led the flock here to Eldey Island and selected the landing site — now assumed undisputed leadership. A powerful, experienced old bird, he marshaled his troops with the pomposity of a heavily medaled general, clucking sharp orders as he swam back and forth along the periphery.

The young great auk was terribly impressed with the old bird and soon followed him everywhere, never

more than a few feet behind. Once or twice he tried
to surge ahead or even swim alongside the leader, but
a stinging jab of the sharp beak drove him back. Except for this, the old leader paid little attention to him,
seemingly unconcerned about anything except the
flock as a unit. His lack of cordiality did not deter the
young great auk and when the old bird was seen,
the young one was certain to be only a length behind.

The second sun of September had just kindled its
red-orange blaze on the eastern foot of Eldey Island
when a piercing trill broke through the general hubbub
of bird calls and sloshing waves. The great auks
turned as one and stared at the old male, who stood
starkly erect with his wings flapping almost as if he
were attempting to applaud, head thrown back and
partially opened beak pointed straight upward. Over
and again the weird trill sounded from his throat.

Another of the adults picked up the call and then
a third echoed. Abruptly the whole flock emulated the
action and voiced the same sound, and the very
strangeness of it caused the other island birds to
silence their own voices and stare in wonder at the
large black-and-white birds.

The young great auk felt the same stirring trill
bubble up in his own throat and he tossed back his
head and let it roll forth, delighted and even a little

frightened by the penetrating vibration of his own voice. Like the others, he waved his wings slowly back and forth and the tips barely brushed against one another on the forward beat.

As quickly as it had begun, the trilling was cut short, leaving behind an eerie quiet in which the muted rumbling of the sea sounded abnormally loud. Gradually the other bird calls began again and as they did so, the flock of great auks followed the old male into the sea. By the time the light of early sun no longer reflected redly from the face of Eldey Island, the great birds were mere specks on the western horizon.

The fall migration had begun.

It is significant, perhaps, that eighty adult birds had arrived at Eldey Island more than three months before and now, despite the hatching of twenty-eight eggs, only seventy-six great auks were there to begin the great journey.

The days passed rapidly with an almost unvaried routine. Determined strokes of legs and wings pushed the birds westward with a steady untiring pace for hours and days on end. The old male led the flock and the young great auk swam almost on his tail. Now and then he would attempt again to swim abreast the old bird, but received only a sharp jab from the leader's beak as a welcome. The rest of the birds formed a great oval-shaped flock behind them.

Occasionally one or another of the adult birds in the van of this oval would dive and be lost from sight for long minutes. Eventually, however, the bird would pop back to the surface in precisely the same position it had vacated for the dive. Most often it would remain silent after the dive and simply swim along with the rest, but occasionally it would chuckle gratingly and the flock would slow. Only then would the old male dive, arrowing mysteriously to the exact spot where a school of food fishes twinkled through the water, flashing the unmistakable silver of their sides.

The old bird would swim far to the side of the school, pacing it but not approaching near enough to alarm it, studying its size and direction. Then, his wings trailing at his sides, he would cup the water in his big rubbery feet and virtually run to the surface, bursting through with a raucous screech that would send all the birds into an instant dive.

As soon as the feeding was completed, the flotilla would head west again, murmuring happily at their full stomachs and with the lingering excitement of the chase.

The young great auk was thrilled with the vastness of the sea around them. Far from any land, the water had taken on a deeper green tone and the increasing coldness of it lent a joyful briskness to his movements.

Herds of porpoises were seen with unusual frequency and their rising, blowing, rolling and even leaping were soon accepted as commonplace. Once, however, the young bird was fascinated and a little frightened by a great herd of perhaps two hundred seals that intersected their line of swim, causing the birds to slow down slightly until they were past. The seals had come from the northeast and were heading southwestward. Where they had come from and where they were going was a mystery.

Now and again a migrating flock of flying sea birds would flash past, stirring the great auks to a chorus of screeches and raspy calls which were answered with chirps or chucklings or equally grating calls from the fliers before they passed out of hearing. Once in a while such flights would circle the great auk company several times as if hopeful the bigger birds would drive to the surface a school of herring or capelin. These birds seldom stayed long, driven ever onward by their own relentless migrational urge.

The days fused in an endless and untiring motion to the west. There were times when the flock would slow — though never quite stop — and actually seem to be moving as robots, hypnotically, silent, steadily ever westward. During such somnolent periods the birds rested and regained strength, even though they kept on moving. Each day they covered about thirty-five miles. Few were the outside interruptions to break the monotony, but there were some.

Once a tremendous, ninety-foot blue whale rose like a sea monster from the surface only a hundred yards ahead, filling the cold air with a permeating stench issuing in great clouds from its blowhole. The birds veered slightly but seemed little concerned as they paddled swiftly by, no more than forty yards to the left. Another booming, roaring blow sounded, followed by a mammoth inhalation, and the giant's head and back disappeared, the gigantic flukes rose high into the air and crashed to the surface with the sound of a titanic wave smashing against a rocky bluff. The waves it created spread outward swiftly, but the great auks bobbed over them nonchalantly. The whale did not reappear.

Another time there was more excitement and no little fear. The old male, surging ahead as always with the young great auk directly behind him, stopped the flock with a queer whistling grunt. While the birds milled about he virtually stood on the water, paddling swiftly with his feet to hold him upright, head held as high as possible and keen eye locked on a spot of sea far in front. More than three miles ahead a great bulk lay high in the water, belly up. Similar black-and-white torpedo-like shapes thrashed about it, tearing at its mouth and eyes and flukes.

Occasionally the large shape would raise its head above the water level — identifying itself with the tremendous size of its mouth as a bowhead or Greenland whale — and attempt to shake away the fierce killer whales ripping great chunks from its lips. Soon it stopped all struggling and lay quietly sinking while the killers gorged themselves.

The whale was relatively small for its species — probably no more than forty feet in length. Normally the bowheads stayed quite close to shore for protection from the herds of killers prowling the sea, since they are relatively slow swimmers and defenseless against the black-and-white sea wolves. This individual, however, was in very deep water far from land, perhaps led astray in search of the minute plankton which made up its diet.

The old great auk now settled back on the surface and grumbled warningly. He sank until only a few inches of his neck held his head above the water and the remainder of the flock followed his example. Far to the south in a great half-circle they swam silently, even though now the whale and its killers were gone from sight. The great auks did not look back. The peril past, it was forgotten.

Seventeen days after the migration began, the heavily glaciered bulk of southern Greenland appeared on the horizon. This sight of land — their

first since leaving Eldey Island nearly six hundred
miles behind — thoroughly inspired the birds. Along
these rocky shores would be an abundance of food.
They pushed forward with increased speed.

There was indeed a pronounced increase in the food
supply in the Greenland coastal waters. Fabulously
large schools of herring and pilchard, menhaden and
capelin, as well as various types of rockfish abounded
in the waters. Once more the air above the raft of
great auks was filled with the flying forms of various
sea birds, some of which had undoubtedly left the
Icelandic waters long after the great auks had and
arrived on this vast ice-capped island long before
them.

In some areas the shoreline rose smoothly into
grassy plains extending to the mammoth glacial
plateau, but for the most part the cliffs sprawled
directly to the sea, presenting a craggy, weather-
scoured face to the incessantly crushing waves which
battered it.

The great auks followed the eastern shoreline of
the big island south, their pace more leisurely now,
but never completely stopping. More time was taken
for feeding and the energies that had drained away
during that swim across the open ocean from Iceland
were now replenished.

Frequently the rocks and ledges along these shores

were covered with the large bodies of harp seals which groaned and barked noisily as the flock passed. These mammals were superb swimmers and once the young great auk encountered one at a depth of over thirty fathoms — much to the astonishment of both.

On the third morning after their arrival, when Cape Farewell at the island's southern tip lay yet a day or so ahead of them, the young great auk saw a large raft of swimming birds emerge from a fiord ahead of his own flock. He croaked questioningly and the old male spun in a circle on the water ahead, bobbed approvingly at the young bird and then raised himself high for a better look. A queer pleasing cry chattered from him almost immediately and he led the flock rapidly toward them.

The flock ahead had spotted them now and stopped their forward pace, milling and calling enthusiastically. A strange exultation rose in the young bird's breast as he recognized the flock as another contingent of great auks — the only other birds of his own species he had ever seen besides those of his own flock.

In a few moments the two flocks joined in a wildly swirling mass. There were deep low cries and delighted chirps as the birds bumped gently together, touched beaks and nuzzled one another. There were forty-nine birds in the new flock, including sixteen young birds.

This flock had broken off from the flock in which the young great auk's parents had been last spring on the way to Eldey Island. Led by a badly scarred, one-eyed old female at that time, thirty-eight great auks had cut away from the main flock and selected for their nesting site the protected fiords along this stretch of coast. Their choice had been a wise one, for the vicious storm that had so severely decimated the Eldey Island bird population had not touched this area.

Nineteen chicks had been hatched to the flock and the mortality rate among them had been quite low. Two of the baby birds had been snatched away by a marauding Greenland fox and one had for some reason sickened shortly after hatching and had become progressively weaker until it died. Surprisingly, more adult birds had lost their lives in this flock than young ones. Two had been slain by wolverines and three others had paddled out to sea together and had not returned.

Even with these losses, however, the small flock had increased by eleven birds, which was decidedly good. This group had apparently just gathered and left the fiords of their summer residency for the migrational swim when the young great auk's flock hove into view.

There was no question that they would stay together now, and, after some minutes of the same kind of jockeying for position that had taken place off Eldey Island, the pattern for the forthcoming swim was set. Once more the huge old male from Eldey Island took the lead, although the big one-eyed female stayed close behind him, alongside the young great auk, and occasionally took the lead when he submerged or turned back to swim the fringe of his flock, chuckling encouragement to the one hundred and twenty-five birds in his care.

In another day the flock swung neatly around the tip of Greenland, lingered for several hours to herd into deeper water a large school of pilchards upon which all fed with gusto — accompanied by a crazily wheeling, diving host of other sea birds attracted to the scene — and then headed directly across the mouth of Davis Strait toward Labrador. The old one-eyed female now swam abreast of the old male, but the young great auk was still not permitted to leave his place behind the latter.

Separating Greenland from Labrador and vast Baffin Island, Davis Strait was the source of the frigid Labrador Current and sliced to the north for a distance of fifteen hundred miles. Without the bulk of land to the north to protect them now, the birds swam directly into their first winter storms of consequence.

The young great auk felt the first storm coming hours before it arrived. Instead of great masses of clouds sweeping down from the north, there was an almost imperceptible changing of the sky; the deep blue became less intense and then the northern horizon was no longer blue but an ominous dark blue-gray. The swells turned into small waves and then became larger until the entire flock was sometimes cradled in the great troughs between them.

A primitive fear filled the breast of the young great auk and a strange, pitiful moaning emerged from his throat. The birds behind him picked it up and it became a ghostly dirge from over a hundred birds that was snatched up by the ever-increasing wind and blown away.

The old male and one-eyed female remained calm, occasionally glancing back toward the flock and trilling sharply, but always pumping steadily onward. It was much too far to return to the dubious safety the tip of Greenland might offer. The only alternative was to continue southwestward.

Although the young great auk and some of the birds trailing behind submerged occasionally, they didn't remain under water long and surfaced in the same position they had vacated. The two lead birds did not dive, only increased their pace until even the big young bird had to concentrate on keeping up.

The wind was bitterly cold, a frigid scythe sweeping over the tops of the waves, lopping off their foamy heads and carrying them away with howling whines. It had become extremely dark now and the young great auk, only a half dozen feet behind the leaders, had difficulty keeping them in sight as he bobbed high on the wave crests and swished into the troughs.

The young bird's legs and wings felt leaden. Every so often a wave would loft him so that his wings beat in the air instead of pushing the water, and the lack of resistance slapped the wings stingingly across his sides, weakening them even more and filling the bird with a pervading weariness.

All at once his head was being stung by fierce little white flakes streaking along with the wind almost parallel to the surface. He closed his right eye against the pain brought by the first snow he had ever encountered. It didn't last too long, but for a short span, during which he lost all sight of the rest of the flock, it filled the air chokingly, rasped with savage bite into his nostrils and abated after long minutes when the bird was nearing that point of trancelike exhaustion that had gripped him in the storm earlier that summer.

With the passing of the snow, the wind let up a little and the waves became less difficult to buck. The young great auk caught up to the two lead birds, who had now cut their pace to such an extent that they swam almost leisurely through the water.

The young bird's right eye, closed against the stinging snow, had frozen shut. Time after time he ducked his head beneath the surface and shook it until finally the ice was cleared away and he could blink his eye normally. The slower pace eased the ache in overexerted muscles and the young bird relaxed, feeling a new strength, a sort of second wind come over him.

The other birds began closing ranks now and soon the entire flock was swimming slowly in a compact cluster. No, it wasn't the entire flock. Six birds were missing. Several times the old male turned over the lead position to the one-eyed female and swam back along the edge of the flock, crooning and grumbling. Once he paddled back in the direction from which the flock had come until he was out of sight, but the flock continued swimming easily, regaining the strength the storm had cost them. It was nearly two hours before the old male became a speck on the rolling surface behind them and another half hour before he caught up — still alone — and resumed the lead. He screeched shortly several times as he swam through the midst of the flock and the birds spread apart to give him room for passage, falling in behind as he went.

On the flock swam, at an increased pace now, through the dimming of the gray day and into the night. An hour after darkness had crept over them, another storm — this one short-lived and less severe — buffeted them. Once again, just after midnight, a similar squall hit them. At dawn another of the flock was missing but this time the old male did not turn back.

Food for the flock was a major concern now. The storms and heavy use of energy had sapped the birds to the point where another bad storm could wipe them out. The old male dived time after time in search of fish, as did others of the flock, but this far out in the ocean the pickings were slim.

For thirty-seven hours after leaving Greenland the battery of swimmers continued without pause for rest or food. Late in the day the young great auk dived deeply, streaking easily into the peaceful world below the waves, feeling an enjoyment in being by himself for a brief while. He turned and rose, dived and leveled off, his keen glance searching always that outermost limit of visibility for movement . . . and then he saw it.

Far ahead and only slightly to the right was a great flickering of silver bodies flashing through the gloom. The young bird shot toward the spot and saw before him a fantastically large school of sardines in a great migratory stream. So dense was the school that it was impossible to see through it to estimate its thickness. In appearance it was like a gigantic ribbon stretching out of sight in both directions and fully thirty feet from top to bottom, with the uppermost fish about seven fathoms below the surface. The bird paused and watched this unusual sight. Moving rapidly toward the southwest, the school was an orderly, beautiful, wavering band of silver in the dim gray-green light. In the few minutes the bird watched it was likely that more than a million of the little fish swam past him — and still the rear of the school was not in sight!

The young great auk now churned toward the surface, calculating his distance from the flock and changing direction slightly when he saw the silhouettes of the birds on the surface above him. Directly behind the two leaders he burst through the surface, his body clearing the water and his strong grating call filling the air with a wild excitement before he dropped back to the water surface.

The old male and one-eyed female dived instantly and the remainder of the flock chattered and slapped their wings. The young great auk abruptly realized that he was in the lead. Instantly he uttered a sharp screech that silenced the flock and continued the swim southwestward. Obediently the birds fell in behind him. The young bird's breast filled with a new strength and he thrust ahead with powerful strokes, head held erect with firm new pride.

The two leaders were gone for nearly six minutes. As the young great auk had done, they burst from the surface in front of him with raucous voices stabbing the air. When they dived again, the flock dived with them.

The ribbon of silver still stretched out below without apparent beginning or end. These were the pilchards, fine fat sardines of four to six inches in length, rich in strength-giving oils and fats. The school must have numbered in the billions. The appearance of the birds affected them little, so intent were they upon following their leaders. Instinctively the great auks abandoned their usual practice of driving the school toward the surface. Instead, they swam parallel to the fringes of the school, occasionally plunging into it and then returning to open water to swallow the fish that had been caught.

For over an hour the flock gorged on the sardines, occasionally rising in groups of three or four or ten or twenty for new air before resuming their attack. Still the ribbon of fish stretched endlessly in both directions and though each of the birds consumed upwards of two dozen fish, it was as if the school had never been touched.

When he had become so full he could swallow no more, the young great auk darted along the outskirts of the school and now and then slashed into it, delighting in the way the dense masses parted to let him through. He joined a small group of great auks for a while, then left them to join others in the distance. He scanned each of the birds carefully. His mother was undoubtedly back in the main body of the flock somewhere.

Many times he thought he glimpsed her ahead and sped in that direction, only to find it was another bird. Eventually, when all the rest of the birds had returned to the surface, he joined them. Perhaps he had, after all, just missed her in the milling throng of submerged birds.

When he surfaced the flock was a hundred yards distant, paddling easily toward Labrador, and he quickly joined them. They were content now, the fat sardines bringing renewed strength to tired muscles and the throbbing excitement of the hunt gradually subsiding. The young great auk pumped up through the rear of the flock, zigzagging here and there, his eye stopping briefly on every bird. In a few minutes he had regained his position at the van behind the old male and large one-eyed female.

His mother had not been in the flock.

Not until then did the young bird realize that his mother was one of the seven birds lost in the storms during this crossing of Davis Strait.

A plaintive, chattering cry welled up in his breast and spilled from him into the air, silencing the rest of the birds. There was no answer and the old leaders continued swimming steadily. Almost automatically he followed, but for a long time he saw little of the sea or sky around him.

After an hour or so the old female dropped back from her place beside the old male and swam silently beside the young great auk. From time to time her tough old wings brushed lightly against his. An almost inaudible chirring came from deep in her throat and the young bird answered with the same lonely note. She swam beside him for over an hour and then gradually resumed her position sharing the lead. Once she swiveled her head back toward him and repeated the chirring sound.

The young great auk increased his pace and within a few yards had drawn abreast of the old male, swimming as closely beside him to his left as the one-eyed female swam beside him to his right. Perhaps it was a reward for finding the tremendous school of sardines. Perhaps it was because he had shown he could lead the flock when the two leaders had dived after the fish. Perhaps it was out of respect for his loss.

In any event, the huge raft of great auks now had three leaders.

V

O^N October 14 — forty-three days after swimming away from Eldey Island and twenty-two days after leaving Cape Farewell to cross Davis Strait, the most hazardous stretch of water in their migration — the regiment of great auks climbed tiredly ashore on a gravelly stretch of the coastline of Huntingdon Island, Labrador. This was a turning point for the migration. The westward portion of the journey was completed, as was the crossing of vast open sea. From this point onward they would follow the North American coastline southward and seldom be far out in the open sea. If and when the fierce gales howled out of the north, the coastline would provide considerable protection.

Nine harsh squalls had roared over the raft of birds during its crossing of Davis Strait — only one of which matched in severity the first storm encountered after leaving Greenland. Two other great auks, both older birds and both impaired by old injuries, were lost before Huntingdon Island was reached.

This island was a massive chunk of rock, nearly rectangular and almost twelve miles in area, which guarded the mouth of Sandwich Bay. The waters around it abounded in schools of fine food fish, most of which were seen in migratory patterns heading southward. These schools were not only followed by sea birds and mammals, but were pursued vigorously by predatory fish such as mackerel and cod, ling and haddock, bluefish and striped bass.

It was a new world for the young great auk, for he now saw many forms of land birds as well as sea birds — strange-looking creatures with dainty bills, skinny legs ending in widespread unwebbed toes and fluffy plumage always in need of preening when disturbed by even the gentlest of breezes. Equally unfamiliar were the long-legged shore birds which ran along the water's edge in a never-ending quest for food, or stood statuelike in shallow water, strong beaks poised to thrust into the side of any careless fish swimming past.

Great herds of seals covered some points of these shores and, true to form, filled the air with their deep bellowing and barking at one another. Once in a while they would take alarm and an entire herd would simultaneously toss themselves into the water with a great roaring and splashing.

For several hours after reaching the island, the flock simply stood and rested, enjoying the feel of solid ground under their feet after so long a-sea. Gradually the flock began moving about, many of the birds waddling back into the water to fish. At nightfall, however, they were once more massed together solidly to rest until morning when the migration would continue.

At dawn the birds were afloat again, following the lead of the old male, the one-eyed female and the young great auk. During the night the air had turned bitingly cold and there was an increased tempo now in the southward swimming. At long intervals the birds would slow down and move along casually in the almost sleep-swimming manner, during which expended energy would be built up again. At times the flock would stop for a short time to fish. Most of the time, however, there was an imperative drive in each of them to keep moving to the south before the icy grip of winter closed over them.

Around the hump of Labrador the flock swam, across the narrow Strait of Belle Isle, westward through the strait until it opened into the great Gulf of St. Lawrence and then southward again, still along the west coast of Newfoundland.

They did considerably more submerged swimming here, as occasional small boats appeared along the shorelines. The flock would continue swimming to within a few hundred yards of a boat. Then, at a command from the old male, they would submerge, change direction and swim in a great half-circle, popping to the surface far beyond the little craft and continuing the migration as if the boat had never been.

Cabot Strait, separating Newfoundland and Nova Scotia, was crossed next. Its fifty-mile stretch was as nothing compared to the crossing of Davis Strait. Mostly the weather was sunny, but at times a raw norther struck and the flotilla hugged the coastline for every bit of protection it could offer.

One morning shortly after they had navigated Cabot Strait and begun the three-hundred-mile swim down the length of Nova Scotia, a great clamor of screeches and hoarse cries drifted to the ears of the leaders from the birds in the rear of the flock. The three birds spun about and instantly saw the reason.

Swimming to intersect them at an angle from the open sea to the northeast was an exceptionally large phalanx of great auks. It spread out for more than a mile and its width was over a hundred yards. These were the great auks that had nested and spent the summer and fall on the barren rocky shorelines of southeastern Newfoundland, from Trinity Bay to Fortune Bay.

Numbering over forty-three hundred birds, this was the largest remaining flock of great auks. Yet, large though it was, it was small compared to the great flock it had once been. As short a period as a decade ago this flock had numbered nearly forty thousand and even then was by no means the largest individual population. A community of great auks that had nested on the many tiny islands of Hamilton Inlet of Labrador once was conservatively estimated at well over five hundred thousand! In one year's time — during the height of the breeding season — this flock was virtually wiped out. Less than two hundred birds of that massive population survived the great plague which swept like fire through it, leaving the corpses of the birds scattered over the islands, and even now, years later, the bleached bones and skulls of tens upon tens of thousands of these birds still littered the island like brittle driftwood.

So, while over forty-three hundred great auks was a mammoth flock in its own right and in this year could be considered downright huge, it was actually only a pitiable reminder of the teeming masses of the species that once plied these same waters twice each year.

The young great auk's flock stopped and circled about excitedly, waiting for this new flock to join them. The raspy roar of thousands of deep cries filled the air in an oddly beautiful symphony. In the van was a magnificent three-year-old bird, fully two inches taller and several pounds heavier than the young great auk. His voice was thunderous and unmistakable among that vast chorus and he swam to the three leaders of the little flock without hesitation.

A strange ritual was now enacted as the huge bird circled first one, then another, then the third, all the while uttering a meaningful staccato cry. Three times in succession he swam swiftly around the three birds as individuals, bobbing his head gravely, then twice more around them as a group. The three floated quietly, alternately dipping their heads in return until they brushed the water, then snapping them upward until the beaks pointed straight toward the heavens.

The bedlam of cries from the other birds gradually dwindled in volume until it was hardly more than a murmur and the greatly enlarged armada watched their leaders curiously. The big leader stood high in the water and flapped his flipper wings several times, then disappeared beneath the surface, leaving behind scarcely a ripple to show where he had been. At once the old male and the one-eyed female performed the same movements and disappeared beneath the surface. The young great auk did the same.

Far ahead and below he could see the big leader being followed closely by the pair from his own flock.

He streaked after them and followed in a strangely intense type of follow-the-leader. Down and down the big leader pumped until darkness had cut even their keen subsurface vision to a dozen feet or so. Here, almost forty fathoms deep, the pressure was tremendous and enveloped the young great auk's body in a crushing grip.

An enormous rock lay ahead, forming a natural arch with another rock of smaller size, and through this narrow opening the big leader swam. There was so little room that even though he pumped only with his feet, his sides still brushed the walls of the archway as he sped through. The two older birds followed without hesitation, as did the young great auk. Another great rock — actually an undersea cliff — loomed ahead and the big leader swam toward it at a phenomenal speed. Collision seemed imminent when he angled sharply upward, his brilliant white belly feathers barely brushing the rock surface as he ascended vertically with tremendous pumping kicks of his splayed feet. Both the old male and female emulated the maneuver, though their approach to the cliff was not as swift and the veering upward to avoid collision was begun a bit sooner. The young great auk, however, flashed through the water every bit as swiftly as the big bird had done, rocketed upward at the last possible moment and felt a jarring impact as his belly slammed against the wall and continued to slide along it as he continued his ascent. Only with the greatest of effort did he manage to pull away several inches, his muscles straining dangerously with the effort. The big bird had widened the gap between himself and the two older birds, while at the same time the young auk had narrowed it. Soon he sped past the two and even cut down the distance between himself and the big leader.

Now the latter turned on his back and swam upside down with firm, measured strokes, quite as smoothly as he had been swimming right side up. The young great auk also turned over but his strokes were not as sure and his body tilted from side to side with the unusual posture.

At length the big bird turned over, stopped, released a sizeable bubble of air and sank in a gentle lifeless spiral. The young great auk also turned over and stopped but, with his bubble of air released, he became alarmed at how little a reserve of oxygen he had. He allowed himself to start this aimless fall but abruptly gave it up and scrambled for the surface, bursting through in a great jump and filling his nearly empty lungs in a tremendous wheezing gasp. Despite the great amount of energy used in this weird contest, he had been under water for just over eleven minutes!

The two older birds bobbed quietly on the surface nearby. A moment later the big leader surfaced with no more of a commotion than when he dived. Unbelievably, he seemed little pressed for air. The two old birds nodded their heads vigorously and after a moment the young great auk did the same. The big bird raised high on the water, shrieked stridulously and headed southward. The two older birds and the young great auk — all three still abreast — fell in a few feet behind him. None of the four looked back but they knew the large flock was following them and that the last half of the migration was under way — with an indisputably powerful new leader.

With the prevailing winds at their backs and the sea running calmer now that they were in the lee of Nova Scotia, the great auks made excellent time. Regardless of their stops for catching food and periods of sleep-swimming, the birds still averaged better than thirty-six miles per day. Most of the time they swam about a mile out from shore, although there were times when they came to within a dozen yards of it, or when the coast was barely visible to them, as when they crossed Mahone Bay.

The big leader did not appear to have any great fear of small boats and, since the craft they had seen thus far had shown no interest in pursuing the birds, they seldom dived when passing them any more. They had dozens of them in sight at once as they passed

Halifax, including some very large four-masters with their sails filled like overstuffed feather cushions and heading seaward.

The young great auk was fascinated by all the boats and when one was within sight he found it difficult to tear his eyes from it. Even the smaller boats with their long spidery arms that dipped and rose, dipped and rose, were highly interesting.

It was on the fourteenth day after the two flocks had merged that the birds approached Cape Sable at Nova Scotia's southernmost tip. Ahead of them were five of these small boats lying nearly motionless on the flat calm water surrounding them. There seemed little to fear and the birds continued their pace without hesitation.

As the phalanx drew nearer, however, they could see that the boats were pulling apart somewhat and forming a wide half-circle into which the flock must surely swim if it kept upon its present course.

The big leader slowed, his nervousness apparent as he circled several times, always turning back to the boats now less than two hundred yards ahead. The bow of each of these boats was pointed toward the flock, and the opening of a three-inch black pipelike instrument jutted from each bow.

Slower and slower became the forward movement of the huge flock, and then the leaders came to a standstill as strange sounds issued from the boats.

"You men ready over there?" a coarse voice shouted from the middle boat.

"Yo!"

"Ready!"

"Aye!"

"Ready!"

"Steady now," came the call from the middle boat. "All at once when I say three. Here we go now . . . One . . ."

The rear birds were catching up to the stalled fore-section, tightening the flock into such a dense mass that the water was scarcely visible in the sea of black-and-white birds.

"Two . . ."

The old male at the young great auk's side suddenly flapped high in the water, a long strident shriek bursting from him.

". . . THREE!"

Five explosions almost as one blasted out from the small boats and the air around the flock was filled with screaming bits of metal — bent nails, pieces of chain, lead balls, jagged bits of iron.

In the very act of turning back to the water to dive, after his warning, the old male flopped spasmodically as a jagged chunk of metal tore away most of his skull. Dozens of other birds at the same time screeched and thrashed as bits of deadly shrapnel sprayed about them, many pieces passing through two or even three individual birds before lodging in another.

There was no time to look about to see the result. As if it had never been, the flock disappeared beneath the surface and at a depth of forty feet sped out toward open sea in panic-stricken haste. Here and there as the birds winged and pumped through the clear greenish waters a bird would weaken, fall behind and begin to rise, a tiny cloud of red misting the water from the spot where it was wounded. At least four of the birds lost their air and sank, disappearing gradually and forever into the dimness below.

Not until they were more than a quarter mile distant from the boats did the birds resurface. Even then it was only for a moment to replenish their air for another long dive. Twice more this was repeated and when finally they resurfaced and did not dive again, the boats were mere specks behind them.

For long hours afterwards there was a desperate haste in the birds to put many miles between themselves and the treacherous Cape Sable. One hundred and seventeen great auks were missing. Another twenty-six still with the flock were wounded — five of these seriously. Six hours after the slaughter, these five had died and seven others had fallen back until they now formed a pitiful little flock of their own, limping painfully after the main body of birds, unable to comprehend what had happened, knowing only that they were hurt and tired and could not keep up with the rest despite increased effort. By the time darkness came, they had fallen back almost out of sight and in the cold light of a dull gray morning, as the massive raft of birds finished crossing the mouth of the Bay of Fundy and hit the Maine coast at Bar Harbor, the seven had disappeared. None were ever seen again.

Except for one fact, this incident was simply another dreadful lesson of life to the leaders. The exception was a fact which took the birds a long time to comprehend — that the wily old male was gone permanently. For days after the incident the young great auk and the one-eyed female swam as far apart as they ever had when the old male swam between them, almost as if they expected him to reappear at any time. Only gradually did this distance close and not until they had nearly completed their journey across the island-studded mouth of Penobscot Bay did they swim as close to one another as they had to the old male.

The hundreds of islands along this Maine coast provided excellent fishing for the travelers, including a far greater variety than any of the younger birds had ever before experienced. There were still the bounteous schools of herring and pilchard, capelin and menhaden, but now there were fine large schools of shad fingerlings entering the ocean from the rivers and estuaries where they had hatched and grown to their present length of three or four inches. There were great schools of silversides, too, their mirrorlike seven-inch lengths flashing like wind-blown aspen leaves in the waters relatively close to shore. Their meat was rich in oils. There were also the delectable American smelt, most of them about eight inches in length but some schools with individuals reaching up to a foot in length.

Following these schools of southward-moving fish were many species of predatory fish — including the cods and bluefish, striped bass and pollack and mackerel — all determined to have their share of the bounty. Not infrequently they found themselves snatched up by a great auk or a razor-billed auk or one of the other sea birds, provided they were small enough.

One day while slicing through the water to attack a school of capelin, the young great auk spied a squadron of mackerel also driving into the mass of fish. Instantly selecting a fifteen-inch specimen as his target, the bird changed direction. The mackerel lost interest in the school and put on an astonishing burst of speed, accompanied by erratic maneuvering to elude the big bird. He was no match for it, however, and before the chase had gone more than a few hundred yards, the strong beak of the bird clamped across his back. A swift jerk of the young great auk's head broke the fish's spine. Returning to the surface with his catch, he found it quite an abundant mouthful but managed to get it down, although for more than an hour the end of the tail hung ludicrously from his mouth.

After passing Casco Bay and its great harbor city of Portland, the shore topography changed drastically. The massive cliffs and boulders which had formed the only shorelines the young great auk had known up to now were replaced by stretches of long sandy beach, casually studded with large, half-buried rocks. The air was full of gulls which seemed to find this extensive raft of birds of unparalleled interest and hovered above them for long hours, screaming and laughing and often diving to skim just out of reach over their heads.

Steadily the migration progressed and the skies became consistently less clear and the sea less calm. Gripping cold winds slashed in from the Atlantic and the sky remained such a monotonous leaden hue that it seemed almost to promise never to change back to its previous blue.

The flock rested little. By now the leg and wing

muscles of the huge birds had become accustomed to the interminable pumping and they could continue without tiring.

At Cape Ann, Massachusetts, a certain confusion resulted when the big leader and one-eyed female struck out southeastwardly to open sea instead of following the shoreline as they had up to now. The young great auk issued a grating protest and circled vigorously, turning several times to go back toward land.

Grunting in a low tone, the two leaders continued to swim in their new direction. After a few minutes of indecision, the young great auk joined them, swimming as usual beside the old female and the two of them only slightly behind the big leader. For two days they were out of sight of land while the leader continued unerringly on his course.

The afternoon of the second day showed far ahead on the horizon a long low spit of land — a great arm jutting into the sea. This was Cape Cod. Had the birds followed the shoreline as the young great auk had indicated they should, they would have had to swim more than three times the distance to get where they were now.

Around Race Point the flock swam and down the great sandy beach that rimmed the Cape Cod shoreline. Sharply southwest they turned at the Cape's southeastern tip and paddled through Nantucket Sound between Nantucket Island and Martha's Vineyard. With so many boats dotting these waters, the birds stayed far from shore and permitted no boat — large or small, rowed or sailed — to get within a half mile of them. Several times it became necessary to make wide detours around small boats that turned toward them and attempted chase. The painful memory of the five little boats off Cape Sable was still fresh, and they made every effort to prevent a recurrence of what had taken place there.

The birds passed Long Island on November 14 in the midst of a howling storm which thrust at them from behind for three days, lending even greater speed to their strokes. On the eighteenth of that month they navigated the wide mouth of Chesapeake Bay and swept slightly southeastward along the narrow stretches of sandy, scrub-grown beaches separating them from Currituck Sound and Pamlico Sound. They clung rather closely to the empty shore now, pumping easily around the point of Cape Hatteras, and were at last on the homestretch.

Less than an hour after turning around this point and heading almost westward in the lee of that great outcropping of land that marks the North Carolina coast, the flock encountered another — and final — contingent of great auks which had arrived here nearly a week before. This flock had just over seven hundred birds in it and, as the two flocks mingled, there was a general happy chuckling and the miseries of the long migration behind them were wiped away.

The pace slowed and groups of birds began to separate from the main flock. Here, two hundred birds dropped out — and there, another hundred. A little group of ten swam shoreward and another group of fifty merely stopped and played lazily in the clear azure waters, inspecting this different world surrounding them where the water was warmer than it ever became in the far North Atlantic and the air was as balmy as the warmest day of summer on Eldey Island.

Some of the great flock continued in a desultory manner to the southward, but by November 26 all had stopped and taken up winter residency on that long stretch of northeast-southwest shoreline stretching from Cape Hatteras to Cape Lookout and from Cape Lookout to Cape Fear — eighty-six days and nearly three thousand miles since the young great auk had left Eldey Island.

It was a good site, as few boats traveled these waters and the possibility of danger from landward was remote. The fall migration was over and the flock had been reasonably lucky. With the joining of the Newfoundland flock off the northern coast of Nova Scotia, the population had leaped to over forty-four hundred birds. Despite the encounter with the boats, the loss of wounded birds and the disappearance of six others between Cape Cod and Cape Hatteras, the flock still numbered forty-three hundred and one.

Now, with the enlargement of the flock by the waiting birds at Cape Hatteras, there were along this desolate coastline a total of five thousand and two great auks — the final remnants of a population which once blanketed these same shorelines by the millions.

Even though the number was now relatively low, there was no reason to believe the population wouldn't increase gradually to its former numbers, provided the destructive hands of man and nature could be avoided for several years.

While such a small population was noted with alarm by a handful of bird lovers and naturalists who journeyed to North Carolina that winter to see the flock, the birds were unaware of it and basically content with their lot. Life was good here — plenty of food, relatively warm weather and little danger from either man or natural enemies.

It was a peaceful winter for the great auks.

VI

THAT fall and winter was long remembered as one of the very mildest winters on record. Normally the North Carolina coast was brutally lashed by at least a dozen bad storms and two or three full-blown hurricanes, although the hurricane season was generally over by the time the great auks arrived. Nonetheless, the coast in this area did not experience even a moderately heavy blow. The tropical storms that were spawned in the Caribbean either quickly blew themselves out at sea or dived inland on the Florida peninsula and dissipated. Even these were remarkably gentle storms for the season.

The great auks spent the winter in a kind of carefree sociability — hunting the schools of silvery smelt and halfbeaks, capelins and herring that constantly swam these waters, basking in the warm afternoon sun on the long sandy beaches, clustering in small groups for all the world like tuxedoed gentlemen at a garden party, muttering among themselves and waving their wings in extravagant gesticulations to emphasize a point.

For the young great auk it was a wonderfully enjoyable world. Every day brought new experiences, new things to see and smell and hear, new places to explore. He spent many hours waddling along the desolate shoreline, picking up bits of shell here, following little trails there.

Although the long beaches looked quite deserted at first glance — except for the population of great auks, immense flocks of gulls and scattered populations of other avian migrants — these sands were actually alive with a variety of shore life.

Among the scattered shells of long-dead mollusks and silicified wood the young bird watched the movement of this life for hours on end, utterly fascinated by it. Here a little lump of sand heaved and the bird's probing beak uncovered a predatory moon snail hunting for small mollusks which it could drill open and devour. There a V-shaped sand trail was seen and, when the young great auk followed it to the originator, he found a little burrowing clam or a heart urchin or a sea mouse. Often the sand showed a wavering ribbonlike track which ended with the discovery of a small starfish or a sand dollar unconcernedly easing its way along between tides.

It was at low tide when the incredible amount of

life abounding in this seemingly barren shore area was most apparent. Often great flats of sand dozens of acres in area would be exposed, or covered at most by only an inch or so of water. Here the tiny ghost shrimps peeked from their little burrows, ready to snatch what little food particles the water brought their way. Extending several inches above the sand, the plumed worm Diopatra waved its marvelously shell-and-seaweed-bedecked outer coat in the gentle water movements.

The crabs were everywhere. During the night in particular the little fiddler crabs would emerge from their burrows in such numbers that the sound of their passage was like the constant crinkling of paper. There were so many that it often seemed as if whole sections of the shoreline were moving. Sometimes the males would stand for long hours in front of their burrows at the edge of the beach grasses and wave their one oversized pincher claw in a "come hither" gesture meant to entice any passing female. Now and then certain individuals would become alarmed, stand high on tiptoes and scamper sideways to their burrows to escape the danger, real or imagined. The danger was almost as often real as imagined. Large blue crabs prowled the shallows after dark, dashing ashore occasionally to snatch up an imprudent fiddler. The pretty calico crabs — their sand-colored shells splotched in light red bordered by dark lines — were also a hazard for the fiddlers, as were the ghost crabs and lady crabs.

Grotesque but graceful sting rays sent up clouds of sand in the shallows as they nuzzled for mollusks, and here and there in the shallow waters the back of a large horseshoe crab would emerge like some mysterious little primeval monster as the crustacean searched for tiny mole crabs and sand fleas, leaving behind its strange track of two parallel lines between which could be seen a squiggly tail mark.

Where passages of deep water had chewed their way in close to the shallows there was constant activity. Here the larger predatory fish flashed in and out, feeding on the sand eels which were, in turn, feeding on the little silvery salt-water minnows that dashed through this treacherous area in great nervous clouds.

So the desolate beaches were not really desolate at all. Shore life was everywhere. Wherever the young great auk explored — whether high on shore where the dunes began and the beach grasses held the sand from being blown away, or on the water's edge where the tide was actively working, or in the vast acres of inch-deep shallows, or even on the edge of the abrupt drop-offs from crystalline beach water to the dark blue-green of the deeps — the presence of myriad life forms was visible. It was a wild, beautiful, unforget-table world of nature.

By the end of February, after three solid months of feeding, relaxation, exploring and leading a gener-ally complacent existence, the young great auk was undoubtedly one of the three largest birds of the entire population. Standing upright, his head towered a full thirty-four inches from the ground — nearly half a foot higher than the average. He had become strikingly handsome, his plumage tight and thick and lustrous against his body and in many ways more like a beautiful black-and-white fur coat than a mantle of feathers. The large oval spot between eye and beak had now become startlingly white and a badge of authority held high over the other birds.

As the early winds of March paced warmly up those great beaches a certain nervousness became evident in the birds; in just a few of the older males at first but then quickly spreading to the others. Small groups, then larger ones swam out to sea almost out of sight of land and floated there facing north, feel-ing a faint but unmistakable pull. The very atmos-phere seemed to carry a message to them that it was time to go home, time to return to those bleak but compelling cliffs and rocks of the far North Atlantic.

Several times the big leader from the Newfound-land flock stood erect, waved his wings and gave voice to that weird trilling call. It would be echoed here and there by individuals, including the young great auk, but gradually the flock would settle down again and lose interest. It was not yet time.

Not until only nine days remained in March did the full and undeniable migrational urge sweep over every bird, and now when the big leader raised his call it was echoed throughout the flock and the birds began massing. By late in the day over three thousand had grouped together — and as the sun hung only inches from the western horizon, a large cluster of birds that had gone farther south between Cape Lookout and Cape Fear hove into view. Perhaps this was what the flock had been waiting for.

The big leader and the young great auk swam out to meet them, followed at a respectful distance by their own huge entourage. The raft of birds from the south, led by none other than the old one-eyed female, numbered nearly two thousand. There was much bobbing of heads and circling of one another among the three leaders while at the same time the two large flocks mingled and a happy, conspiratorially raspy greeting rose in a muted din over the quiet coast.

The big leader dropped his head so that a great arc formed in the ebony neck and the tip of his powerful beak just barely touched the water. The young great auk and the old female did the same and without further exhibition the three set off abreast of one another. The flock fell in behind, and in this manner, as the light of a ruddy full moon shimmered the water low over the Atlantic, the northward migration of almost five thousand great auks began.

For some reason he could not quite comprehend as yet, there was a far greater urgency in the young great auk's breast for this migration than for the one that had brought him here, strong though that one had been. It was as if at the end of the swim there was waiting for him something terribly important, something which beckoned him irresistibly. That this same feeling was widespread throughout the flock was evident in their eagerness to swim at a rapid pace which seemed as though it should quickly expend their strength, but did not.

Before the moon had trundled very far across the sky, the great flock wheeled around the point of Cape Hatteras and struck out due north. Unlike the southward migration, their way now did not cling so closely to the shoreline; they often spent days at a stretch out of sight of land, seeing few boats.

Not until their northward course intersected the eastward jutting shoreline of New Jersey just below the mouth of the Mullica River did they resume the journey within constant sight of the shore. Above them flew great flocks of birds of all types — black ducks and eiders and scoters and cormorants, cranes and herons and tiny sandpipers and even small flights of lovely white egrets, long disorderly groups of gulls, streaming graceful columns of pelicans, vast clouds of blackbirds and orioles and tanagers and swifts, high-flying and gracefully gliding pairs and foursomes of bald eagles and various hawks, plus hundreds of others ranging in size from diminutive chittering songbirds to huge buzzards — all moving northward, seeking the answer to that same obsessional pull that drew the swimming birds.

Again came those periods of feeding on the schools of herring and pilchard and capelin also heading north and times when that strange somnambulism took hold of them and they slept and rested, even though their limbs continued to move methodically and their directional sense never faltered. The feeling of intense need to get "home" was not appeased by each day's miles put behind them but only seemed to increase, igniting them to a feverish pitch hardly containable. Even the brief stops for feeding were often cut short — the call from the north stronger than all but the greatest hunger.

With Long Island and Block Island behind them, the raft of birds swam to within half a mile of the Rhode Island coast, crossed the quiet mouths of

Narragansett Bay and the Sakonnet River and then cut directly eastward across Buzzards Bay. Few, if any, humans saw the mammoth flock swim through the narrow passes between Naushon Island of the Elizabeth Islands chain and Woods Hole on the southwesternmost tip of Cape Cod, for the passage was made in the middle of the night while a reasonably heavy sea was running. By dawn the flock had passed across Vineyard Sound and were out of sight of land again as they navigated Nantucket Sound.

It was late in the day when they reached Monomoy Point and swung northward, once more close to shore but again hidden by darkness. Throughout the night they swam steadily just beyond the outermost breakers that rumbled shoreward on the great expanse of sand beaches from Chatham to Provincetown.

They paused only once to fish along this stretch of beach during the early morning hours, and the abundance of schooled fish enabled them to catch their fill rather quickly. It was during this dive that one of the great auks near the trailing end of the flock disappeared. The young great auk, alerted by the frightened murmurings of the rearward birds which were echoed forward until they reached his ears, turned back and chattered consolingly, calming the uneasy flock. The birds continued swimming but the young bird dived. For long minutes he flashed through the turbulent water in ever-widening circles. He saw many schools of small fish and several large individual fish, but no signs of the missing bird. He surfaced for air and dived again. Still there was no indication of what had caused the disappearance.

A strange sensation, almost of panic at some unseen but strongly sensed menace, washed through him momentarily and he sped to the surface. By the time he overtook the rear of the flock he had recovered himself. He chirred softly again to the birds as he passed them and resumed his position at the lead. Here he muttered softly and the old female and big male cocked their heads for an instant but continued their unbroken pace. The incident was over. It was soon forgotten.

Several hours after nightfall the flock left behind them Race Point at the northern tip of Cape Cod and drove northwest across Massachusetts Bay. It was nearly noon of the next day before the bulk of Cape Ann greeted them. They widely skirted numerous boats heading toward or leaving the fishing center of Gloucester and continued swimming far out from shore, despite their hunger. Since the majority of schools of small fish followed the shorelines rather closely, the several brief fishing stops that had been made by the flock en route across the big bay had been basically unsatisfactory. Therefore, soon after rounding the tip of Halibut Point, when one of the flock, a dozen or so birds behind the leaders, popped back to the surface from a dive with a frantic screech, the young great auk and the big leader dived simultaneously. They saw the school of capelin instantly, but it was disappointingly small and heading swiftly toward a huge rocky bluff jutting from the shoreline which provided ample hiding places.

The two birds ignored the little school and continued forward, skimming close to the bottom just over five fathoms deep. The big leader gave up the search, turned and streaked back toward the surface to rejoin the flock. The young great auk continued the underwater flight alone.

Far ahead, a slight movement on the bottom caught his eye and he beat his way in that direction. There, struggling as if they were hurt in some manner and unable to flee, were three small scup — bluegill-like fish of excellent flavor. Without hesitation the bird dived to the attack and snatched up the first fish, which seemed uncommonly heavy and struggled only weakly in his grip. He swallowed it and began to turn back to the other two when he saw they were trailing behind him, attached to a thin dark line which disappeared into his own mouth. Suspicious, he started swimming away and was halted sharply as the fish in his stomach leaped back into his throat and hung there for a moment. Off to the side on the bottom behind the trailing scup, a heavy, smooth object bumped along.

Alarm shrieked in the young bird's brain and he tried to regurgitate the fish he had swallowed, but it held tenaciously in his throat. He jerked harder and something tore from the fish, slid up his throat and then painfully stabbed through the very corner of his beak.

This was the young great auk's first experience with a fishhook and very nearly his last encounter with anything. Frantically he shook his head and pulled against the heavy drag of the big sinker but he could neither break loose nor pull the heavy weight to the surface.

His air supply — which had been nearly expended when the big leader turned back to the flock — was now perilously low. His struggles became more frantic and the hole made by the hook was enlarging as the flesh at the corner of his mouth ripped. The bright red of his own blood in the water spurred him to a tremendous effort to break away. He felt the jaw skin tear even more and then the hook fell free from the flap of loose skin hanging from his chin.

A dire blackness was beginning to close over him as he bulleted to the surface. How sweet the taste of air in those great lungs! For long minutes the bird gasped and sucked at the air — but even through this, his legs instinctively carried him away from shore and the insidious danger lurking there.

His jaw burned terribly as the salt water washed through the wound, but the bleeding quickly stopped and the sharpness of the pain became a numbing ache. The flock, closer to shore than was he, was nearly halfway past him. He paddled slowly until his breath was coming normally again and then he increased his pace to catch up with the leaders. It had been a nearly disastrous encounter with a fisherman's trotline and he would never have another. He could not know that he was one of the fortunate few great auks to escape drowning that had found themselves in similar predicaments over the years. It was a lesson dearly learned and he never again trusted the sight of helpless fish on the floor of the sea.

The injured jaw remained sore for many days but the bird had remarkable recuperating powers and before long it had healed nicely. Perhaps his beak could not grip with the power it once had but there was still sufficient strength there for him to snap up the pilchards and herrings and other small fish making up the bulk of his diet.

Once again they were traveling the inshore waters where schooling fish abounded and the flock fed well.

Several days after the fishhook incident, a smashing spring squall ripped the shoreline two hours after nightfall and forced the birds — for the first time since leaving the North Carolina shores — to coast to the beach on great breakers and huddle together in the shelter of massive rock clusters jutting from the sand. The storm lasted for over three hours and provided a welcome respite for the birds from the constant moving of their limbs. Even after the blow was over they stood quietly for more than an hour, dozing and regaining spent strength.

They crossed the mouth of Casco Bay, with the Maine shoreline now more rocky than sandy, on April 12. It was a beautiful morning without the trace of a cloud anywhere in the sky. The ocean, which this far north usually took on that cold gray-green tinge, seemed startlingly blue under the early sky. There was only enough wind to cause light flurries of ripples to dance over the surface, catching the sun and reflecting it like the bursting-through of a school of skittering silversides.

The birds were in a gay and playful mood on this bright day and their raspy voices grated back and forth through the flock in an almost constant companionable hubbub. They dived at random, a dozen here, three or four there, perhaps half a hundred in another spot. There were times when as many as a quarter or a third of all the birds would disappear for a short while and amuse themselves chasing young gray pollack among the rocks below and occasionally catching a fish of ten or twelve inches which was gulped with great relish.

Only the one-eyed female did not dive. Steadily onward she churned, setting the pace for the rest of the flock and barking crisp orders to move them along and hold the ranks reasonably tight.

As they neared the northern tip of Maine's large Damariscove Island, the big leader dived, taking the young great auk with him almost as if the latter bird were pulled along on a string. Playfully the big bird — still just a shade larger than the young bird — sailed through the water executing neat turns and breath-taking dives into the shadowy realm of rocks and moss a dozen fathoms below.

The young great auk followed the leader in every move but made no attempt to overtake him, holding his pace to about a dozen yards behind him. Unexpectedly the big leader flashed over a strange object, slammed into a tight turn and went back to investigate. A cratelike object made of slatted wood rested at a slight angle on the bottom with a long line running toward the surface from the top. It was open on one end.

With his fishhook encounter still relatively fresh in

his mind, the young great auk was filled with instant apprehension at the sight of this line more than at the sight of the strange device to which it was attached, and he kept a considerable distance away, circling slowly around the big leader.

In the bottom of the box lay a chunk of dead fish at which several six-inch pollack were tugging voraciously. The big leader eyed these fish and then sped to the attack. Through the open end of the device he streaked, but the little fish wriggled away through the slats before he could reach them. The big bird turned to cut them off, but mysteriously found his passage barred by slatted wood. Round and round he turned, but always the way was barred. The fun of it all was quite gone now, and the big bird slammed his body frantically against the wood blocking his progress. The box rocked slightly with his efforts but did not reopen.

The young great auk came closer, swimming in a tight circle around the box only three feet away. The big leader tore savagely at the slats with his beak and small slivers of wood filled the bottom, along with clouds of silt stirred up from the ocean floor. The young bird also gripped the wood, but it was heavily waterlogged and defied the most concerted onslaught.

Now the young bird felt the need for new air — but if he needed it, what of the big leader? The need for oxygen grew more and more pressing but still the young bird stayed nearby, desperately frightened at the leader's predicament, unable to help but reluctant to leave.

Eventually he swam upward, knowing that if he were to make it to the surface safely even then he would have to hasten. He burst into the air with a resounding squawk, refilled his lungs and returned to the lobster trap. The big leader lay ominously still on the bottom, his beak locked on the unyielding wood of one of the slats.

The young great auk nudged him but there was no answering movement. A half dozen birds from the flock now came to the scene, including the old one-eyed female. They, too, poked at the big bird with their beaks, circled confusedly around the slatted box and now and then stopped to pull determinedly at the thick wood.

Eventually the old female swam off, angling toward the surface and followed by all but the young great auk. He remained with the trap until his need for air became acute. With a last long look at the dead bird and a gentle nudge at him with his beak, he turned and pumped to the surface.

The flock was several hundred yards to the north when he reached the surface — and now, for the first time, the young leader made no attempt to regain his position in the van. For several hours he swam silently with the rear guard, refusing to join in the lingering gaiety which persisted throughout the flock. Only when the wind began to freshen and scudding soot-gray clouds appeared on the horizon did he speed up and resume his leadership.

The old one-eyed female was leading the flock and he swam to her blind side as usual, and matched her pace. She swiveled her head to look at him, bobbed gravely several times and then concentrated on the swim still before them.

Good leaders are never abundant. The loss of the big bird was a real tragedy to the flock, despite the competent leadership still exhibited by the old one-eyed female and the young great auk. Perhaps if the big bird had lived the events that were to follow might have been greatly altered. Perhaps not. At any rate, the flock continued northward, the need to get "home" flaring ever more strongly in their breasts.

VII

THE great auk became undisputed leader of the flock shortly after the death of the big leader in the lobster trap. It was not a sharply defined transition from his role as associate leader with the old one-eyed female, but more or less a gradual acceptance by the flock in general and the old female in particular that this huge strong young bird was the individual to be followed.

The big bird fitted into this new slot smoothly and, while the female still swam at his side and he gave close attention to her actions and indications at various points of the journey, it was clear that the decisions for flock action were basically his own.

Only one other bird in the huge armada was as large as the great auk. This was another male of several years whose right leg was badly knobbed at the ankle where it had once been broken when he had stepped into a crack in a rock and stumbled. Large though he was, this bird seemed altogether content to remain back in the flock with no inclination to be a leader. At the moment, in fact, he was considerably more interested in the two-year-old female swimming demurely at his side than in anything else.

The same attitude, to a lesser or greater degree, was being evidenced by a large number of the great auks. In the majority of cases this was taking place between pairs of birds that had become mates the previous spring or in seasons before that. Once mated, an auk never paired with another. The yearling males and females — or those older that had not previously mated — kept fairly well to themselves, though their glances flicked slyly over one another now and then. Only the older birds whose mates had been slain or had disappeared in one way or another maintained a stolid aloofness, concentrating only upon swimming and feeding. Such birds might, if the parents of a fledgling were killed, adopt the orphaned bird. Mostly they kept to themselves, content in swimming along northward with the flock.

The great auk himself several times shot meaningful glances at the old female at his side, but there was absolutely no response, nor would there ever be. Eight years old — which was by no means ancient, but certainly a respectable age for an auk — the old one-eyed female had many seasons before been mated to an aggressive male her own age, for two years. Together they had raised two chicks, only to see both of them killed — one by a great horned owl on the coast of Labrador, who himself was killed by the attacking parents but not before his talons had gouged out the female's eye; the other during a freakish hailstorm when lumps of ice the size of plums had smashed into the flock while it rested on shore, killing nearly half the birds in those dread three or four minutes the hailstones pelted down. The young bird had withstood those that struck his feather-padded back, but three of the stones, almost as if directed, smashed into his head — the first stunning him and the next two in rapid succession crushing his skull as he lay helpless. There had not been another chick to the pair after that because in their third season together, while en route to the nesting grounds, the male had been shot down along with several others when he waddled ashore on the eastern end of Long Island.

The great auk quickly realized that he would not be accepted as mate by the old female and he contented himself with pushing onward to the north. At Bar Harbor he led the flock almost directly eastward across the mouth of the Bay of Fundy and, when the southern point of Nova Scotia appeared on the horizon, he kept the birds several miles from shore until they had traveled well around the treacherous Cape Sable. All along the Nova Scotia coastline, in fact, he held the raft of birds at least a mile from shore, although the schools of food fish were more difficult to find so far out. Not until they had gone across the wide mouth of Chedabucto Bay to the Cape Breton Island portion of northern Nova Scotia did he allow them to come close to the shore again.

It was at Cabot Strait that the first indication of dissent to his leadership came. The great auk automatically turned north here to travel up the Gulf of St. Lawrence along the west coast of Newfoundland, just as he had come south. The majority of the birds, however, had not initially moved south via this route and indicated their desire to strike out northeastward along the southern coastline of this roughly triangular island. Many of them had been hatched or had raised their own chicks among the hundreds of islands in Bonavista Bay on Newfoundland's east coast under the big leader. Had that latter bird still been with the flock there is little doubt that it would have gone in that direction.

The great auk, however, was not to be led aside here, nor would he idly permit any challenge to his authority over the flock to go unanswered. While the one-eyed female continued to lead the way northward up the Gulf of St. Lawrence, the great auk churned back and forth along the perimeter of the flock, squawking imperiously and occasionally even nipping at the recalcitrant few who attempted to swing away from the main flock here.

Eventually the birds settled down and once more docilely accepted the great auk's authority. The big bird resumed his place beside the old female and the migration moved along well. Into the narrowing Strait of Belle Isle they swam, crossing over now and swimming close to the wild shore of southern Labrador.

Shortly after turning north along the east coast of Labrador, a group of fifty-five birds separated from the rear of the flock and headed in toward the many rocky isles of St. Michael's Bay. Resolutely they ignored the angry cries of the great auk and even though he pursued them and tried to turn them back to the main flock, they resisted. These birds were led by a rather small male bird who, despite their difference in size, clashed with the great auk in a melee of slapping wings and stabbing beaks. This was *his* little flock and he would brook no interference.

Eventually the great auk turned about and headed back to the large raft of birds, dismissing the small contingent from his mind. In a few moments he had regained the lead. Here he stood high on the water and screeched loudly, then settled back and led the flock onward at an increased pace.

They passed the great herds of harp seals sprawled lazily in the sun on the rocks but paid little attention to them. The occasional passing porpoises were always carefully eyed to make certain they were not killer whales and, when indisputably identified, they too were ignored.

Where the hump of Labrador began to curve north-westward toward Sandwich Bay, the big bird struck out confidently to the east northeast. Over the flotilla flew intermittent flocks of gannets and jaegers, puffins and razorbills, heading in the same direction to nest on the barren outcroppings of southern Greenland or Iceland or even as far east as the clustered Faeroe Islands. Their journeys across the bleak six-hundred-mile mouth of Davis Strait would be finished much more swiftly than that of the great auks. These same birds would undoubtedly be perched happily over their eggs by the time the great auks saw them again.

Now and then little flights of puffins or dovekies or razorbills would set their wings and swing in a wide circle about the raft of birds and then settle to the water and swim with the flock for a time, perhaps even joining them in their dives for food. They never stayed very long, however. Although they could not long keep up with the constant, rapid swimming speed of the great auks, this was still much slower than their own flight could carry them and the pull of the mating grounds was too urgent for them to tarry.

Nature smiled on the flock during this crossing of the icy gray-green strait, for only two relatively light storms struck and none of the more than forty-nine hundred birds was lost. At one point a dense fog merged sea and sky into an eye-straining, palpable gray mass. Almost immediately several migrating flights of gannets, puffins and razorbills dropped to the surface and swam along with the great auks, though off to the side. None of them, however, could match the driving pace — not even the close razor-billed cousins of the great auks — and they were soon lost behind in the mists.

For three days the fog clung, becoming progressively denser, enveloping them like a clammy blanket. In one respect it was a blessing. As long as the fog held on, the sea would remain calm, heaving in great swells but without wind to cause the peaked waves which took such effort to swim through. Shortly after dawn on the fourth morning of the fog a breeze freshened from the north and soon the mist had blown clear, leaving behind a brilliant blue sky and a mildly choppy sea.

On May 24 — sixty-three days after leaving Cape Hatteras — the armada of great auks rounded Cape Farewell on the southern point of Greenland and forged northward along the bleak shoreline. The abundance of schooling fish here was fantastic and it was seldom that any individual of the flock had a stomach long empty.

The evening of the second day after this turning point, the great auk led the flock into the sheltered water of Danells Fiord after a particularly large school of menhaden. Then a strange thing occurred. Although the great auk planned to lead these birds back to his own island of Eldey, they broke ranks and swarmed shoreward, led by none other than the old one-eyed female, screeching and moaning delightedly. It was not an unpredictable happenstance. The great majority of this flock had been hatched on Newfoundland's east coast and now they were far beyond that point. They were ready and eager to stop here for their nuptial ceremonies. A large portion of those that had not come originally from Newfoundland with the big leader had come from this very fiord area last fall with the old female and, as far as they were concerned, this was home. The small remaining group of birds — only a few over fifty — that had come from Eldey Island were bewildered and milled about in the water, muttering querulously.

The great auk had come to think of this raft of thousands of birds as his own flock and responsibility and he could not now simply set off without them, trailed by only a relative few, back to Eldey Island.

The pull of that island was strong in him, but not so strong as his desire to stay here with the main flock. Therefore, after only a brief hesitation, he raised his head and trilled loudly. The remaining cluster of birds broke up swiftly, most of them heading toward shore.

The great auk did not immediately follow. Taxed by the demands of his leadership, he had burned great amounts of energy and was very hungry. He slipped beneath the surface twice and fed voraciously on the silvery seven-inch menhaden. At length he swam purposefully toward shore with one of these fish gripped crosswise in his beak.

It was a craggy shoreline here, and appeared to be an ideal nesting site for the great auks. There was only one area on the cliff face rimming the fiord where the great auks could land. This was a sloping rocky shore between sheer bluffs which led upwards from the water rather steeply, quickly changing to a foundation of solid rock. This rock rose in wavelike swells to a height of perhaps eighty feet above the water where it ended in a rock-walled dead end. There were several clefts in the cliff edge which permitted the birds a view of the sea and rocks below, but for the most part it was a neatly sheltered undulating plateau protected on all sides from the weather and basically inaccessible to invasion from land predators. A more ideal nesting location, it seemed, could hardly have been imagined.

Coasting inward on a bulging swell which broke just before it reached the slope, the great auk held his fish high and paddled gently until he felt the slippery rock beneath him. He let the water carry him as far as possible and then waded beyond it as it began to recede. It was not Eldey Island but, for this season at any rate, it would be his home.

A dozen feet up from the water he stopped and peered about himself. Little clusters of great auks were everywhere, some claiming those accessible niches and wall crevices, but most of them standing guard over bare spots of rock which looked like any other bare spots except to the bird or birds presently guarding it.

As the plateau climbed higher, the numbers of birds thinned, and it was in this direction that the great auk now wobbled like some ridiculous clown, appearing all the more foolish with the silvery fish flopping lifelessly in his beak at each rolling, unbalanced step.

Several times he saw females with one or two or three males standing before them, bobbing and swaying and softly crooning, but he passed them by. Occasionally he saw young females standing alone, but for some indefinable reason he did not approach them.

Then, far ahead, he spied a handsome female not much smaller than himself. She stood in the entrance to a sheltered tentlike niche of a cliff wall, unimpressed by the wing-flapping and awkward excitement of the male who stood a few feet in front of her.

The male became more and more enthusiastic, evidently tremendously impressed with his own beauty, his own fine baritone voice, his own graceful movements. What a distinctly charming bird he was and what a fine catch for some unattached female like this! He was not even disheartened when he lost his balance, tumbled over and rolled down the slight incline for eight feet before stopping. Doggedly and as passionately as ever he lumbered back to the female. This time, however, he came injudiciously close to her and her boredom gave way to a streak of irritation as she jabbed him sharply in his immaculate white breast with her beak. So strong and unexpected was this thrust that the startled male was taken off balance and once more tumbled over and rolled down the incline. His dignity, when he scrambled to his feet this time, was slightly punctured and he grumbled deeply in his throat. This was a fine way for a lady to react when being so grandly wooed by so noble a character as he.

While all this was taking place, the great auk waddled up and the difference in size between the two males was quite noticeable. The great auk stood nearly five inches taller than this courting male and his general build was much broader, his carriage more assured. Pointedly ignoring the smaller male, he paced to within three feet of the female and stopped. For long moments they stared at one another, motionless as statues, her glance tinged with faint suspicion and his indisputably phrasing a question.

With a barely audible rasp spilling out past the fish in his beak, he gave his head a short sharp jerk and paused, watching the female closely. For a long moment she did nothing and then there was a slight but visible relaxing on her part. With a movement so imperceptible that only the closest scrutiny would have caught it, she dipped her head. The great auk saw it.

The rasp in his throat now spilled out in a deeper joyful cry and he flipped the little fish five feet into the air over them. The female followed the arc of its fall and caught it neatly. She held it half in, half out of her mouth for a full minute. With a sharp bob of her head she snapped it in two and swallowed the anterior half while the tail portion cartwheeled through the air. The great auk snapped it up and almost lost his balance in the process. The morsel disappeared down his throat and he turned quickly to face his rival. The latter, still grumbling audibly, was already waddling back toward the sea. He was going fishing!

The great auk and his mate stood for a long while together in the little chink of the cliff, rubbing their beaks against one another's neck and wings and breast, occasionally embracing with their narrow wings.

Abruptly he shook himself, and in that instant the female dropped submissively to the ground. The great auk followed her and there was a peculiar moaning cry from both as the hunger that had sparked within him as far back as Cape Hatteras and had built up during the migration to the passionate fire now coursing through his veins was temporarily appeased. Six days in succession they mated in this manner — always in the same place, always at the same time of day.

In the days that followed, most of the great auks traveled about on land or in the water in pairs. There was one group of perhaps thirty or more birds which stayed together nearly all the time. These were the old birds, both males and females, who had lost mates or the young males who had been unsuccessful in winning a mate during the courtship proceedings, since there were more males than females in this flock. These mateless young males did not appear at all disconsolate at their poor fortune but fished and frolicked in the water, stood chuckling in compact clusters on the shore and generally seemed to be enjoying their bachelorhood. Always at the head of this group, of course, was the large old one-eyed female.

The great auk and his mate had an egg.

It was a beautiful thing and its owners were as proud as any two birds could be. The great auk spent his days waddling to the water, fishing, and then waddling cheerfully back up the long slope with gifts for his mate. She never snatched the fish from him but merely sat calmly on the egg until he stopped beside her. Then she would touch his breast with her beak and nuzzle her neck and head against his in obvious enjoyment before finally reaching out and delicately accepting the prize. Once in a while the great auk would keep the egg warm while the female fished, but not very often. She could not seem to keep herself away from it for any length of time.

On the day when the incredibly ugly little fledgling weakly shook off its shell and sprawled miserably on the ground in the cleft, the great auk went wild. A tumbling, thrilling scream burst from his beak like a trumpet call over the thousands of nesting birds, repeated again and again. He virtually ran in crazy bumbling shuffling strides to the cliff edge and recklessly thrust himself out, knifing into the water fifty feet below and only clearing a rocky outcrop by a scant inch or two.

His dive carried him far beneath the surface and then he raced back up and burst through, tumbling back into the water with a mammoth splash unlike his usual neat, almost rippleless dive. He turned in sharp circles and then chased his tail head over heels, sinking all the while, until he looked like an oddly revolving black-and-white ball spinning down into the darkness of the deeper waters.

He chased fish and snapped them in half without bothering to eat them and he encountered a huge halibut which sped seaward in terror away from the weird apparition. The great auk chased it, cut it off, circled it and confused it so badly that it soon hung motionless on the bottom, gills pumping with exhaustion. The bird left the fish only when the need for air became too acute to ignore any longer.

For an hour he continued this wildly exuberant display without tiring, and then he finally began fishing in earnest and returned to his mate's side with an eight-inch herring which he presented to her in an almost courtly manner.

The newly hatched bird was a female and unspeakably repulsive. The sooty black fuzz covering her stood straight out as if she were perpetually scared to death and her big mouth seemed never to close. At first the female regurgitated great gulps of half-digested food from her stomach to feed the little bird, but gradually this food became less and less digested until the little bird was swallowing chunks of raw fish and whole little fish with gusto. She would eat all her parents brought and often her little stomach was so distended that it seemed another speck of food must surely cause it to burst. By the end of two weeks the little bird was as large — though scarcely as attractive — as a small chicken.

The schools of fish seemed to enjoy Danells Fiord as much as did the great auks and other sea birds nesting nearby, for there were always clouds of tens of thousands, even millions of sardines and herring and capelin constantly following the rim of rocks near the shore. Food was never a problem and the weather, despite recurring heavy fogs, was extremely mild. It seemed the gods were showering the great auks with blessings.

Then came the boats.

The two three-masted ships moved into the fiord silently with the early light of dawn and anchored no more than a hundred yards from the gravelly slope leading to the great auks' nesting plateau. The birds that could see the ships stared mutely, uneasily, but as yet without fear.

Seven longboats — three belched from one ship,

four from the other — pushed off toward the landing slope. Six of these boats carried eight men each and the last had only seven. All seven craft arrived at the slope about the same time and, with much thumping of oars and bumping of clubs and rasping scrape of ropes over gunwales, tied up securely to the rocks. Wide planks were then laid from the near gunwales to shore and made fast so they would neither tip nor slide free. Then the tall hunters shouldered their thick short clubs and paced up the rolling steplike plateau.

A hazy, scarcely remembered vision from his own youthful days rose now to fill the great auk with a trembling dread. Instinctively he turned to his mate and offspring, waddled toward them rasping softly and forced them back to the farthest recesses of their chink in the cliff. He stood with his back to them, heavy and solid on widespread feet, resolutely facing the opening of the cleft no more than three feet in front of him. His wings jerked slightly and a chattering angry sound bubbled deep in his throat.

The men laughed and called to one another as they paced through the thick population of birds.

"Eh!" shouted one, roughly pushing aside two great auks blocking his progress uphill. "What I tell you, eh? What I say? I say this year the garefowl come back like ten year ago, eh? I say this year we make money, eh? Black-and-white money standing there, black-and-white money. We make barrelful of money this time, eh?"

The others laughed and one called back, "Not so big as ten year ago, Christian. Then there were ten time so many. But, like you say, good flock this year. Plenty garefowl here. I guess you know when you say you know."

By this time the men had mounted the uppermost slope of the plateau, above most of the nesting masses below. The cliffs on each side formed walls thirty yards apart and the floor of the unusual plateau slanted to the sea with a flat surface here for twenty feet or more and then a sharp slope to a similar platform. So it continued its downward levels until it dropped into the gray waters.

Twelve men had remained with the boats and now the forty-three who had climbed the plateau spread out in a line several feet apart from cliff wall to cliff wall. Jabbing roughly at the birds with their clubs, they began herding the masses before them toward the boats.

Now and then one of the birds would scramble through the line and the men would hoot good-naturedly at one another for letting it get past. They made no concerted effort to stop these individuals, however. One in ten, perhaps, squeezed through in this manner, but the majority were pushed onward by the pressing mass of birds and men coming toward them and were forced to move toward the sea.

"If you got to hit, hit head, not body," Christian shouted above the screeching. "Broken heads are good birds. Broken backs ruin meat and feathers, lose money, eh?"

The noise from the great auks increased, but still they were cries more of anger at being separated from their offspring than calls indicating any real panic. A number of the young birds unfortunate enough to be in the way had already been stepped on by the men and either crushed or severely crippled. Their plaintive, fearful cries were almost lost in the deeper roar from thousands of adults.

Halfway down the slope with a solid blanket of birds moving before them, one of the men lost his balance and fell when he stepped on a young bird. Before he could regain his feet nearly thirty of the big birds had waddled through the gap, determinedly heading back toward their nesting sites. Twice in passing, angry birds had pecked savagely at him, and as he stood up he wiped a welling of blood from his cheek with the back of his hand. He was fortunate not to have lost an eye to the sharp beaks.

"Aaaagh!" he roared and his club flailed wickedly. The sound of the blows was a heavy thumping and grunting and at each blow a big bird slammed to the ground, crushed and quivering.

"Eh, Gunnar!" called Christian. "Why you kill them here, eh? You like to carry them to boats? We have enough to carry later on, eh? Push them. Push them. We kill them soon enough, eh?"

The lower birds now became fearful of the boats toward which they were being pressed, and abruptly faced about. The action was repeated by more and more of the birds until nearly all were facing the club wielders. Just that quickly the movement changed direction and the press was now uphill. Here a large group broke through the line of men .. and there ... and there, until the hunters were surrounded by a waist-high sea of black-and-white forms.

"Stop them! Stop them! Drive them back before we lose them and got to start all over!"

All the clubs were swinging now and the screeches of anger were gradually drowned out by the cries of agony from injured birds. It was many minutes before a semblance of the original line of men was regained and the press toward the sea re-established. By then many of the great auks had gotten through and waddled in stupid confusion back to their nest sites where they circled aimlessly and screeched in grief and bewilderment for their trampled or missing young. Several of the adults flung themselves from the clefts of the cliff and sliced out of sight in the water below.

Now the lead birds of the flowing blanket had reached the planks and the boatmen were ready. The birds tried to walk directly to the water, but were thrust back with long knobbed poles and directed by them onto the planks. Inanely they waddled across them to the boats, where they were smashed down as soon as they crossed the gunwales.

On they came and on, totally confused, each seeking leadership out of the dilemma and each finding it only in the senseless following of the bird in front of him. And as this bird's skull was crushed beneath the blow of a short club, the following bird would continue to waddle forward, thrust to the killing place by the mass of birds behind. So they followed and pushed as if intentionally seeking the surcease of this terror which only death could bring.

At one point, while midway across the plank to the boat, one of the great auks lost his balance and fell into the water, instantly diving beneath the boat and out to sea. At last they had a leader! The next bird followed and the next and soon the entire line of birds was rushing forward eagerly to dive.

Cursing, the sailor dropped his short club and snatched up the long knobbed pole. Ignoring those birds already on the plank, he shoved it against the breast of the bird just about to follow the others onto the wood. It was an effort to hold him there, but he managed to do so until the last of more than a dozen birds on the plank had dived. Then he raised the pole and brought it down with great force on the head of the bird he was holding back, and the bird fell to the rock at the side of the plank and lay twitching.

The press of the flock now thrust a different lead bird forward and, guided by the long knobbed pole, he mounted the plank and waddled toward the gunwale. He reached the end all too soon and the others followed him dumbly. The sailor dropped the pole and went back to work with his club. Before an hour had passed, the small boats were filled to capacity and the men in them chanted in unison through cupped hands:

"Back-oh! Back-oh! Back-oh!"

A man's voice from above drifted through the cries of the birds:

"Full up down there? Full up?"

"Full up! Back-oh! Back-oh!"

One of the men driving the flock whistled shrilly and waved his arm and the line of men fell back. They turned and walked back up the slope, mopping their brows on their sleeves. Hot work and the hard part was yet to come.

The men in the boats now beat the planks with their clubs, frightening the birds away from the water, turning them, sending them back. No longer pressed from

behind, the great auks pivoted and wobbled awkwardly back up the hill.

The boat men drove them on and the birds scattered
as much as possible as they scrambled uphill. Now and
then some of the birds would thrust themselves out
over one of the clefts in the cliff to the water below
and succeed in escaping, but more often than not their
bodies would slam with crushing impact against the
rocks below which stretched out too far for them
to clear.

Now the wretched carnage began in earnest. Fifty-
five men there were and fifty-five clubs and the
clubs rose and fell almost methodically and each time
they fell another great auk died, its skull shattered.

Hour after hour the massacre continued. Three
times the men stopped to rest, blocking with their
presence the routes by which the birds might escape,
while the birds waddled as far away from the men as
possible, which could never be far enough. Then the
men rose to their feet, pocketed their pipes and waded
through the pitiful mounds of bodies scattered everywhere. Again the terrible tune of *swish-thump* . . .
swish-thump . . . *swish-thump* commenced.

At least half a dozen times the legs of this hunter
or that strode by the chink in the cliff where the great
auk and his family were couched. Each time, the big
bird fluffed his feathers, swelled until he almost

doubled his size and nearly filled the small cavity, but the men never stooped to peer into the dimness there. Enough birds were here, enough work.

By degrees the screams of the dying birds faded away as their lungs and hearts ceased to function. The awful *swish-thump* lost its metronomic quality, became erratic — a flurry of the ominous sounds here and again over there and then silence, followed by a single *swish-thump* here and another there and again over there.

The men crouched on their haunches now and re-loaded their pipes, breathing heavily and not talking much, individually pleased with the thoughts of the money this day's work would net them. They smoked and talked softly, and their soft words seemed jarringly loud now that the voices of the great auks were silenced. Their laughter was frequent and heavy.

Long after they had knocked the dead ashes from their pipe bowls they rose to their feet and returned to the boats. There was now only room for two men in each of the boats to row back to the ships. The heavy cargo caused the longboats to ride deeply in the water and they were a long time getting there. Men from the ships lowered baskets on ropes and the carcasses of the great auks were tossed into them and then lifted aboard to be dumped into great piles on the empty deck, and then the baskets were lowered again

to the longboats. When the emptied boats returned
to shore, each carried four men instead of two.

Now came the work of picking up the carcasses of
the birds from where they had been felled, and it was
hard labor. The deep sack each man carried could
hold only seven or eight of the big birds and it was
necessary to fill it up, carry the bulging bag weighing
one hundred and twenty-five pounds or more back to
the boats, dump it and return for more. The men
shouted jovial sympathy to one another. Oh yes, it
was hard work. These birds were lucky they never had
to work so hard. They lead a lucky, easy, carefree
life, these crazy birds that stand still and let you
break their heads!

As the carcasses of the adult birds were retrieved,
more and more of the ugly black fledglings became
visible. A great number of them were already dead.
Many more were badly injured and occasionally cried
out in faint little peepings. Others were unhurt but
frightened and hungry and they raised their shrill
voices now and again. But mostly there was a silence
broken only by the clumping of heavy shoes or a
coarse laugh or a guttural comment.

It was getting on toward evening when one of the
men stepped on a little dead fledgling. He stopped,
glanced down and then picked it up. This was the man
called Gunnar and he grinned as he hefted the pullet-

sized carcass. Abruptly he drew back his arm and sent the body sailing through the air. It smacked into the back of Christian's head. The latter muttered a startled oath, spun about and then laughed when he realized what had happened.

"Hah! You want to play bird game, eh? I play too!"

He snatched up the carcass and flung it back at Gunnar, immediately stooping and picking up another fledgling lying near him. This he threw, too. The first bird missed when the hunter ducked, but the second caught him full in the stomach. The other men joined in tossing the little birds, laughing uproariously as they filled the air with tumbling fledglings.

Several times baby birds were thrown which peeped in terror as they whizzed through the air, but the peeping always ended when the little body struck a man or the hard ground. And what difference did it make if they killed them? There were plenty of these crazy birds, weren't there? Hadn't their fathers and their grandfathers and even their great-grandfathers done the same time and again before them? Sure, there were always more.

The throwing game rapidly degenerated into a kicking game and now the men turned into overgrown boys delightedly kicking at the animated black lumps of fuzz on the ground, seeing who could kick them highest or farthest. The best ones to kick, of course, were those which were still able to stand up on their hindquarters, because these would loft high into the air and plop to the ground dozens of feet away in a broken heap. After all, the men had worked hard. All day they had worked hard. Let them have this little bit of fun. What could it possibly matter to anyone?

Soon the burst of fun-spawned energy left the men and they settled back to their work of rounding up the remaining adult carcasses. There were not too many left now. A full load for one of the seven long-boats was roughly one hundred birds. All day long the boats had been filled and laboriously rowed back and forth between ships and shore. Each of the boats had already made six round trips and now, in the growing dusk, the boats were loaded a final time, several without quite a full load, and rowed out to the ships while the hunters squatted near the water and relit their pipes and talked of the stupid garefowl and of the North Atlantic and the money they would make and their homes and their families.

The boats returned after a time and the men loaded up the planks and the clubs and themselves and shoved away from the slope. It was good to be done with the day's work. They had done a fine job and had a right to be proud. Tonight, those on board the ships who had had things easy while the men on shore wielded their clubs would have the job of cleaning the birds — lopping off heads and feet, skinning them and tossing the heavily down-feathered pelts into these barrels and the salted carcasses into those barrels and the heads and feet and entrails back into the sea for the fish. It would probably be an all-night job, this clean-up task, but think of the fine down cushions that could be made from the pelts and the bellies that could be filled with the meat, even though it tasted rather fishy and had to be sold more cheaply than other fowl.

A gentle drizzle began falling as the boats disappeared in the gloom toward the big ships, where lanterns had now been lighted and hung to guide their weary hunters home. It rained most of the night and where the run-off water slid down the declivity it had become a curiously pink color by the time it drained into the sea.

On that single day in June, over forty-eight hundred adult great auks were slain.

VIII

THE great auk did not leave the little hollow in the cliff wall until long after sunup. The rain had ceased while it was still dark and at dawn, when there should have been the all-pervading gabble of shrieks and chatters and trills and hoarse cries from the nesting great auks, there was only a chilling silence occasionally broken by the far-distant barking of a seal or the blowing of a porpoise or minute whisperings from high-soaring birds. The only sound from the plateau was an infrequent shrill and plaintive peeping that could come only from a fledgling great auk.

The big bird's own offspring had twice cried out loudly in the silence. Except for what her mother had been able to regurgitate from her own stomach to feed her, she had had nothing to eat for over twenty-four hours. In a baby bird's life, this is a long time indeed.

The great auk wobbled cautiously and with some stiffness from the cleft and stood for long minutes peering all about him. There were none of his species on the plateau above him, but on the gently dropping slope below were seven great auks, three of them hunched solitarily along the cliff walls and four in a cluster perhaps thirty yards from the water. The overall barrenness of the rocky declivity in all directions was startling, because for weeks this same area had been a seething mass of jocular creatures in neat tuxedos with scarcely walking room between them. The lack of birds now made the plateau seem considerably larger than it had looked before.

The only unnatural thing besides the absence of the great flock was the deplorable number of tiny black mounds scattered all over the surface of the rock. Occasionally one of these little mounds would jerk spastically and even more rarely one would weakly raise a head and open its beak with a tinny cry. These were the pitiful remnants — the dismal legacy — of a race of noble birds. These were the fledgling great auks.

A vast majority of the infant sea birds were dead. Most of the remainder were very near death and would succumb before many more hours elapsed. These were the injured, the broken, the crushed little forms which somehow managed to cling tenaciously to that faint spark of life, though with ever weakening determination. Those few that had not been injured were hardly in better condition. The all-night rain, gentle though it had been, had drenched and chilled them thoroughly and it was virtually certain that none of them could survive this extreme exposure. None did. By midday, of the more than twenty-four hundred baby great auks that had hatched less than two weeks before, all but three were dead.

One of the remaining trio was the great auk's own hungry little offspring. The other two were also female chicks that had miraculously survived in the midst of that carnage and had been found by their parents less than an hour after the boats had sailed away. Both sets of parent birds had been among those that had luckily dived from the plank during the herding of the birds the previous morning. The chicks, warmed under the thick furlike down of the mothers, were in excellent condition now. They had quickly dried and the chills that had gripped them for an hour or so had passed away.

Those three adult birds huddled dismally along the cliff walls had also been among those that had escaped the plank. Throughout the night they had waddled among the pathetic little bodies, seeking their own. They had been unsuccessful. Only one of the three was a female.

As the great auk waddled carefully down the slope, the other adults watched him silently. When he neared the clustered four they rasped a warm welcome and waved their wings slowly. He answered with a similar sound but did not stop. He plunged into the water without hesitation. How grand it was to get back into the water where his heavy body felt so streamlined and as light as a fluff of down.

The big bird submerged almost immediately and spotted a medium-sized school of capelin before his first breath was expended. In and out he flashed, taking only the smaller fish and swallowing them the instant he caught them. He had to surface once for air but immediately renewed the assault. Within ten minutes he was unable to swallow another fish.

Quickly he paddled back to the slope and started the long pull upwards to the cleft. Again the foursome chattered as he passed but this time he did not answer. At the entrance to the tentlike chink, the female and their little chick stood eagerly in the morning sunlight and the little bird squawked anxiously as he scuffed to a stop before them. He lowered his beak nearly to the ground and, with a single convulsive heave, regurgitated the seventeen small fish he had swallowed. Swiftly the female snapped one up and dropped it into the gaping mouth of the chick. A second, third and fourth followed this one. Three more and the little belly of the bird was solidly distended. Now the female jabbed at the remaining fish for herself and in moments had swallowed them all.

She croaked deeply and rubbed her beak against the great auk's shoulder.

The big bird turned and started down the slope. Now the foursome of birds below had increased by two as the male birds that had been hunched by the cliff walls joined them and stood murmuring softly a few feet away. The parent birds had no objection to the company.

Since the lone female leaning against the wall was closest to him, the great auk waddled up to her first. He grumbled but she did not respond, her beak pressed deeply into her breast feathers, eyes closed. The leader touched her with his beak and drew back swiftly when he felt the unnatural stiffness of her. She was quite dead.

The cluster of six — plus two fledglings — greeted him as he approached them with wings flapping and a chirring trill bubbling from his throat. They stood close together for several minutes, wings moving slowly and echoing the leader's voice. When he moved away toward the water, only the two parent females stayed behind to tend their young.

Out in the water the great auk led them in a wide circle first along the near shoreline of the fiord and then across to the far side. After they had fed from a school of capelin, he led them along the rock-rimmed shore and paused frequently to stand high in the water and screech piercingly, his voice echoing back and forth across the fiord from the rock walls.

High above, the jaegers and petrels and fulmars heard the cry. In clefts and crannies the puffins and dovekies heard the cry. On ledges along the fiord shores the crowds of murres and black guillemots heard the cry. A high-gliding great black-backed gull heard the cry and instantly changed direction. And in a sheltered pocket of water between two immense boulders nearly a mile away, a flock of large black-and-white birds resting there heard the cry. Their own chatter stilled and their heads cocked toward the sound. When it came again, one of the birds stood high in the water and answered it with a similar but shriller voice. This bird had only one eye.

The old female eagerly surged out of the pocket into the main body of the fiord, followed by seventy-seven great auks — the sole survivors of the disaster except for the remaining eight adults and three chicks of the plateau.

The reunion was a joyful one. The birds thrashed through the water to reach one another, acting as if they hadn't been together for months. There was excited milling and calling, beak-touching and gentle bumping when they met. The horror of the day before seemed already far in the past.

With the one-eyed female at his side, the great auk

headed back toward the plateau. Twice on the way he dived, and the second time he surfaced he rasped curtly. The entire flock dived then, and swiftly they forced a small school of pilchards to the surface. The water churned with skipping fish and the flying birds drove in by the dozens to join the feast.

As quickly as it had begun, the feeding was over and the birds pumped easily back to the sloping plateau. The risen tide had swept away the bodies of those birds crushed on the rocks below as they had plummeted from the ledges, and now, except for the tiny black carcasses scattered over the rock and the lone adult female leaning against the wall and appearing more asleep than dead, the entire incident might never have happened. What was past was past and life went on, however feebly.

Now came nature's clean-up crews — the great black-backed gulls, each fully as large as the great auks themselves. Boldly the big birds bounced in on the air currents like flying puppets and alighted apart from the great auks who stood in a protective ring about the two chicks. The great auk's chick was deep in her hollow with the entrance carefully guarded by his mate.

The gulls seemed to materialize from nowhere. Probably not more than a dozen gulls of this species had been seen on any one day since the great auks had arrived here. Now, as if an imperative message had been flashed — as indeed it had, with the great auk's cry — they sailed in from all directions. Within an hour after the first bird had landed, snatched up a dead chick and taken off again to disappear to the south, over a hundred of the powerful birds had arrived. The air vibrated with their deep laughing cries of *"Ha-ha . . . ha-ha-ha . . . ha-ha . . ."* and less frequently the short barking cry of *". . . keow . . . keow . . . keow . . ."*

In and out the big gulls sailed all day; and each time one left, a dead baby great auk dangled from its strong beak. The next day the gulls came back again, and the next. By the end of the fourth day not a single dead chick remained on the plateau. Only the dead female, who had now tumbled to her side along the far wall, indicated that anything unusual might have occurred.

Nature had wiped her slate clean.

The chicks grew rapidly and in early July the black fuzz began to be replaced by the same dense swimming feathers the adults wore. The general ugliness of the three chicks gradually disappeared and a promise of their future handsomeness was evident in the strengthening of the beak, the intensity of the clear brown eyes, the flow of the neck into the streamlined body.

Because of the scarcity of chicks, it seemed that nearly all of the birds in the flock felt as deeply attached to the trio as did the real parents. It was not unusual, for instance, for one of the other adult birds to waddle from the water with a little fish gripped tightly in its thick beak, carry it to the trio — who now constantly stayed together — and flip it into the air toward them. Seldom did the fish hit the ground.

By mid-July the young birds were almost fully feathered and, with all the boundless determination of youth, they had explored every nook and dip of the entire declivity. The great auk eyed them proudly. In another week they would be ready for the water.

While he sleepily watched the youngsters wobble back and forth with flamboyantly awkward movements, his keen ears suddenly detected the sound of a strange muted clank. Instantly he stood erect, head cocked, every fiber of his body in a posture of intent listening. The sound came again and the great bird shuffled swiftly to the high cleft overlooking the fiord. Far to the east, just entering the mouth of Danells Fiord, was a sleek white schooner. Her pointed clipper bow cut through the water cleanly, and even at this distance the great auk could see small man-figures on her deck.

The bird's shriek pierced the air and nearly all of those auks presently on the plateau wobbled, slipped, tumbled and scrambled toward the water. Within a few minutes these birds had slipped easily beneath the surface. All that remained ashore were the six parent birds and their three chicks. The chicks were too young, still too unfledged to risk taking them into the water. They would be unable to keep afloat for long, nor could they swim on the surface or below it well enough to escape the danger. No, they could not yet leave the rock and the parents would not leave their chicks. The great auk and his mate moved to keep their chick between them and crouched slightly to shelter her. Thus they poised silently and watched the gleaming craft slip ever nearer, until quite close to the plateau it dropped anchor. The voices of men floated gently across the water.

"My word, doctor, they *are* great auks. I wouldn't have believed it."

"Yes," replied a higher voice, "but unfortunately not in the numbers we'd been told about. I still find it very hard to believe that two ships could have salted down nearly one hundred barrels of great auks from this one fiord alone only a few weeks ago. These stories always become so exaggerated! The birds simply aren't found in such numbers any more. These are the very first I've seen in several years and you know I've been searching for them."

"I see six big ones and two . . . no . . . three little

ones," said a third voice. "That little one on the left was nearly hidden by the two big ones leaning over it. Nine birds in all. That's not very many. Are you still going to take some?"

"Good heavens, man! This is a scientific expedition. What do you think? We've been scouring the shorelines for these birds for months and certainly we're not simply going to look at them now that we've found them. Remember, the museum is sponsoring this trip and they expect results. They have only one mounted specimen and one skin and both, unfortunately, are in rather disreputable condition. It'll be a distinct feather in our caps to bring back specimens like these."

"Well, if they're as scarce as all that," said a deeper voice that had been quiet up to now, "maybe it'd be better to let these alone and look for a bigger flock."

"Captain, I appreciate your concern and it does you credit. However, I am fully aware — completely cognizant, I say — of the scarcity of these birds and have no intention of wiping them out heedlessly. We intend to take only a sampling. And remember," he added after a brief pause, "these specimens will be seen by many thousands of people who might otherwise never see such a bird. It isn't as if we were wantonly slaughtering them for their feathers or meat like those club-

wielding killers we've heard so much about. It's because of men like that that the birds are as scarce as
they are!" He ended his little speech on a high note of
indignation.

"How many of that family group are you figuring
on taking, doctor?" asked the first voice.

"I would say," the doctor said after a slight hesitation, "that one male and one female and perhaps
two of the immature birds would suffice for our pur-
poses. We must constantly bear in mind the unfortunate fact that the birds are indeed scarce and hold
our collecting instincts in tight check. Handsome
devils, aren't they? What a delightful family-group
mounting they'll make. Well, let's get on with it.
Are the guns ready?"

"Yes sir."

"Fine. Now, it's more than likely they'll bolt at
the first shots, so we'll have to make them count. The
adults will be our concern first. The juveniles won't
be able to travel very fast and we should be able to
reload and get two of them as well before they get
away. Now let's see, which adult pair looks best?"

"That looks like a mighty big one hunching down
by that chick on the left, doctor."

"Hmmmm, yes, it *could* be a fine specimen. Then
again, who knows but what it might not be damaged
in some way and can't even stand erect. No, we'll have

to play it safe and try for the standing birds. Those two standing on the far right with the chick a little bit in front of them. You take the one on the left and I'll take the one on the right. I wish now we'd brought those shotguns instead of the rifles, but I didn't really believe we'd get this close. Well, too late to worry about that now. We'll have greater accuracy with the rifles, anyway, but make certain to aim for mid-breast for a quick kill and as little damage as possible to the skins. Now for heaven's sake, don't miss. We may never have another opportunity like this. Ready now? One . . . two . . . *three!*"

Lances of flame shot from the deck of the boat and the two adult great auks to the leader's far left slammed to the ground as if clubbed. The male lay still but the female kicked feebly for a moment.

The other birds scrambled away, panicked at the crashes and the sight of their comrades sprawled in sudden death. The great auk and his mate — their little fledgling toddling awkwardly behind them — headed for an abutment that would hide them from the boat. The other pair and their chick lurched toward the rear wall of the plateau. The frightened chick belonging to the dead birds ran in a bewildered circle, terrified peepings shrilling from its mouth.

The auks had run no more than a dozen or so feet from the dead birds when the thunder sounded again

. . . once . . . and once more. The little confused chick flopped to the rock between its parents, its shattered head coming to rest over the big webbed foot of its mother.

The solid *thunk* of a slug striking flesh close behind him was plainly audible to the great auk. He spun about and nearly collided with his mate running directly behind him. Six feet back their little chick lay on her side, one webbed foot spread wide in the air and kicking rhythmically. Gradually it slowed and then stopped. The great auk shuffled back to it and nudged it with his beak but there was no response. The bright little eyes had already dimmed in death and a scarlet stain spread out on the rock beneath her.

"Look at it!" came an excited voice floating up from the schooner. "Look at the size of that bird! He's magnificent. We *have* to get him!"

The great auk stood still, dazed with the tragedy that had befallen his offspring. Bits of rock suddenly splintered at his feet and he heard the bullet spang away before he heard the actual shot. Swiftly he turned and followed the female, who was now racing along the cliff wall toward the deep cleft that opened to the sea below. On the rim she paused until her mate caught up, then thrust herself far out. Down she plummeted and her breast feathers barely brushed the outcropping ledge an instant before she disappeared beneath the surface. With no hesitation the great auk followed her, striking the water a foot farther out. Deep, deep they dived to the safety of that dim world. They did not surface for a very long time.

The men were disappointed over the loss of the great auk but nonetheless jubilant over their great good fortune in bagging the others. The doctor, a thin man clad in a thick jacket despite the mildness of the day, lifted the dead male by a foot and gloated.

"By Jove, look at this. Perfect. Simply perfect. A clean kill and not much skin damage. Oh, what a fine mount he'll make!"

"This one, too, doctor. A fine female, sir. But, oh my, I'm afraid we haven't had such luck with this little bird. It seems the shot took away most of the head."

He dropped the little bird and strode over to the great auk's chick, turning it over with his toe. "Ah, this one's in excellent shape, though. What a shame, sir, that you missed the big one that came back to it."

The great auk and his mate were just now joining the other great auks that had slipped into the water and escaped. They were nearly a mile away from the plateau.

"Look there, doctor, look! Dozens of them. Great auks, every one."

"By Jove, you're right. Well now, I don't feel so badly about taking them if there are that many. In fact," he fingered his rifle and smiled happily, "I do believe we'd be justified in taking that remaining family group standing over there by the wall, in view of the fact that the destroyed head of this immature specimen just about ruins its value for the museum's collection. Load up, my boy. We're fortunate, indeed. The scientific world will be greatly indebted to us for these specimens. Isn't it a criminal shame, though, that I let that tremendously big one get away!"

The great auks swam under water with only brief surfacing for air until they reached the mouth of the fiord. During one of these few surfacings they heard two rapid shots from the direction of the plateau, a short pause and then a final shot. They dipped under the surface and when next they emerged the open Atlantic was before them and the white schooner was like a little toy innocuously floating on the surface far behind.

That summer the North Atlantic sea birds sailing high over the bitterly cold Labrador Current saw a unique sight — a raft of eighty-two great auks crossing the mouth of Davis Strait from Greenland to Labrador in late July. It had never happened before at this time of year.

It would never happen again.

IX

WINTER's icy-taloned hands gripped the Northern Hemisphere that year in a premature grasp and clung tenaciously. Early in September the temperature fell to record lows in Labrador, hovering below the zero mark for weeks and not rising above the twenties for nearly three months. The fish sped away toward warmer climes and even the hardy seals moved to places farther south than any they had been seen in for decades.

From far north in the Arctic Circle came creatures seldom seen in Labrador. Two great white polar bears one day passed determinedly southward across the mouth of St. Michael's Bay. On the land there were sightings of fluffy white Arctic foxes and, from the tundra, big ptarmigan and goshawks. Even the Arctic tern, who showed little concern in scooping new-fallen snow from its nest, came south ahead of schedule in great clouds that flitted lightly over the waters of Baffin Bay and Davis Strait like the autumn leaves blown over a cobbled Boston street. Great packs of wolves prowled the timber lines and sometimes made expeditions to the very edge of the sea, their feet braced uncertainly against the precarious ice-coated rocks beneath them, their heavy gray coats fringed with an almost perpetual rime of frost.

Lumbering wolverines came too, and black bear and moose, great gray owls and snowy owls. It was a season when even the hardiest of the northlanders were seeking a slightly more hospitable climate for the winter. It was a winter when one might have expected the worst for the remaining great auks during their migration. Even in the best of times their losses had been significant.

After having crossed Davis Strait at the odd time of midsummer, the great auk led his flock back to St. Michael's Bay, where just over two months previously the segment of fifty-five birds had separated from his vast armada to nest on the islands there. At that time, with close to five thousand birds still behind him, fifty-five great auks seemed an insignificant few. Now that same number would almost equal the total remaining birds with the great auk.

The little flock was still there and had fared well in the nine-week interval since they had parted company. Still under the leadership of the spunky little male, the St. Michael's flock greeted the great auk's group with a nonchalance that made it seem as if it were quite the usual thing for great auks to be migrating in midsummer.

The mortality rate among both young and adults in the St. Michael's flock had been remarkably low. Two dozen eggs had hatched and twenty-three of the fledglings had survived and were now donning their full dress tuxedos in preparation for the long swim to come. The single fledgling fatality had come about through accident. On the very first day the little bird had begun to scramble and tumble over his rocky birthplace he had fallen into a small crevice. The more he had struggled, the more tightly wedged he had become. For hours whole clusters of adults had stood in a great circle around this crevice and contemplated the problem gravely. And while they had contemplated, the little bird had grown ever weaker until eventually it just died. The problem thus solved, the birds moved about their business once more.

Four adult birds had been lost. Two simply vanished soundlessly one night and never returned. Another — a rather small two-year-old female — had expired under the talons of a bald eagle. The last, a yearling female, had lost a spectacularly one-sided argument with a black bear concerning ownership of a fish the bird had caught. The outcome had discouraged others of the flock from engaging in similar disputes.

In spite of these losses, the flock had increased from fifty-five birds to seventy-four, and now, with the addition of the great auk's flock, the total had leaped to one hundred and fifty-six.

When any species of creature reaches this low an ebb in population, it is mainly a matter of chance whether or not it will be able to rebuild its numbers. The odds are stacked rather strongly against this happening. Any natural disaster — such as the vicious storm which struck Eldey Island when the great auk was young — could snuff out the species like a match in a gale. A period of concerted depredations by predators can easily whittle away the numbers until the creature no longer exists. Man, with his strange demands for meat or feathers, can swiftly exterminate a species, particularly when its numbers are so hazardously low. Even should the species be so fortunate as to escape the perils of natural disaster, predatory animals or man, another hazard always lurks, against which it is defenseless. This is disease. Silently it comes, striking first one, then five, then a dozen, a hundred, a thousand. If there are enough of the species, some will usually survive to rebuild the population, but when the numbers are so low that the loss of one member is a generic tragedy, the onset of a disease means almost certain extinction of the species.

When almost overnight in southern Labrador the mercury plummeted to a record low — and stayed there — more than a full month ahead of schedule, it betokened an especially severe and damaging winter and boded no good for the remaining great auks.

In one of her queer and unpredictable twists, however, Nature now watched over this valiant flock with great concern. With luck bordering on the uncanny, the raft of birds swam through howling storms and bitterly cold weather all the way from St. Michael's Bay, Labrador, to Cape Ann, Massachusetts, without the loss of a single bird — not even the inexperienced youngsters. All along the eastern seaboard there seemed to be a mammoth increase in the number of boats, but the birds were not once molested or even threatened.

Seldom a day passed when they did not hear — often at uncomfortably close range — the booming of firearms as gunners blasted away at great flocks of black ducks and canvasbacks and other waterfowl moving south. Only once had the spent pellets of a shotgun blast pattered into the water among the birds, but with no other effect than encouraging them into a long and exhilarating underwater swim.

Thus it was that the flock reached that sandy

corner of North America known as Cape Hatteras
without the loss of one bird, without even an injury
to one. It was an occurrence without precedence in
the history of the species.

It was also much too good to last.

As if withdrawing her hand of safety now that she
had conducted the birds to their wintering grounds,
Nature sped away to a point in the ocean off Cuba
where she spawned a little eddy of wind. The eddy
grew to a hard breeze, developed quickly into a
whirlwind, expanded, enlarged, howled defiance at
sea and sky and land and burst its moorings to head
north with the Gulf Stream as a full-scale hurricane.

The great wind roared up the coasts of Florida and
Georgia and South Carolina at an average of thirty-
two miles per hour and the wind velocity gauges
clanked into frustrated immobility when the blast
surpassed their peak measuring ability of one hundred
and forty miles per hour. Once, near Cape Canaveral,
Florida, and again at the Georgia–South Carolina
border, the storm rushed briefly inland but almost
immediately swerved back out to the coast. The full
power of this titanic force then blasted a hideous trail
directly through the North Carolina coast at a point
midway between Cape Hatteras and Cape Lookout.

The flock of great auks had taken up residence just
over a week before on the North Carolina coast at a

point midway between Cape Hatteras and Cape Lookout. The chance encounter was disastrous.

The birds had known for four or five days, of
course, that a great storm was brewing. The sky had
been queer and the tides were wrong — weak when
they should have been powerful and frighteningly
strong when they should have been mild. The flying
birds had flown northwestward in eerie silence, as if
to call aloud would be to give away their presence
and be forced to suffer the consequences. Deep into
North Carolina they flew, farther from the sea than
they'd ever been before. Here they perched like aliens
in oaks or pines or crouched in silence along sheltered
streams or lakes. They were fortunate, for their power
of flight had given them the opportunity to escape
the worst. But what of the flightless birds? What of
the great auks? Still, weren't these the birds that had
weathered some of the most terrible storms the North
Atlantic could throw at them? Surely a storm along
this idyllic coastline would be much easier to bear,
wouldn't it?

It was not.

As the winds picked up speed and the waves lashed
the shore with gathering height and ferocity, the great
auks moved inland, up into the dunes and the dubious
safety of the heavy beach grasses, but the grasses were
flattened and the wind was still only fifty miles per

hour. They hunkered closer and closer to the ground until they looked like so many smooth black boulders jutting from the lee side of the dunes.

Now the hurricane slashed across that long narrow spit of land and in its passage it did many things. Passes were cut through to Pamlico Sound where there had never been passes before and where people had said there never could be. The acres of great shallow sand flats normally covered by an inch to a foot of water now became deep holes as the sand was sucked away as by a monstrous vacuum cleaner. Deep holes which had previously gnawed their way to the very fringe of the shallows now were filled until they were only a foot deep, a half foot, until now they jutted from the water and grew speedily into dunes.

The face of eastern North Carolina was picked up and carried away, sprinkled here and there in a mad-cap manner. Blue crabs and ghost shrimp, octopuses and minnows, jellyfish, clams and large fish were plucked from the water and dropped ten or twenty or thirty miles away on roads or housetops, in swamps and fields. Roofs and clotheslines and fences and out-buildings were plucked from the land and carried miles out to sea. Everything in the path of that great storm suffered.

Including the great auks.

Almost smothering in the sand, yet fearful of raising themselves higher into that grasping wind, they merely waited with a fatalistic calm provided by nature for times like these when nothing is left but the thinnest sliver of hope — and even that sliver is cracked.

The fingers of the hurricane plunged into the dunes and sifted the sand. The roots of the grasses were exposed and tickled by the wind until whole clumps seemed to come to life and jump from their anchorage and spin off into nothingness with the wind.

One of the great auks was pried loose. The wind picked him up and slammed him back to the sand three times in rapid succession and then hurled him out of sight into Pamlico Sound behind them. Two, three, five more came free and rolled like beach balls to the water's edge, where a great gust abruptly lifted them straight up and for the first and last time of their lives they sailed through the air with the weightlessness of birds that actually fly.

More of the birds were torn from the meager shelter and some were rolled and some were bounced and some were blown to the waiting, boiling fury of Pamlico Sound.

The great auk felt those fingers of wind lift him cleanly from the sand and he braced himself for the impact when he would hit ground or water, but it did not come. He sailed with remarkable gentleness —

sometimes on his back, sometimes on his stomach, sometimes slowly tumbling — for many long minutes and then, with the freakishness only a hurricane evinces, was gently deposited on a great mass of sand. A hulking, half-buried object with an opening to the lee of the wind was beside him and his splayed feet cupped the sand and pushed him belly down across the small space and into this opening. The surcease of wind inside was almost frightening. The shelter was a rowboat standing almost on end and buried nearly to its tip in the sifting sands. The quarters were close in the hollow with just room enough for a small sandpiper or sparrow beside the great auk, but no more.

The big bird moved from side to side, drew his legs up and down and his wings in and out and felt himself sinking comfortably into the loose sand for a depth of several inches. He rested his beak on the boards in front of his face. He closed his eyes against the particles of sand which occasionally snapped in with a backlash of the wind.

Amazingly, he slept.

For two days and three nights the great auk stayed in his impromptu shelter and when, on the morning of the third day, he ventured forth, the wind velocity was scarcely twenty miles per hour. He found himself on the leeward side of a huge dune erected by the wind. Looking off from this dune he saw nothing but land and he knew instinctively he was looking northwest. He climbed the dune and at the top saw stretched before him to the south the fifteen-mile-wide expanse of Pamlico Sound.

The waters were still angry and choked with silt, but it was not unswimmable water and he waddled and slid down the dune to the beach. At the water's edge a large redfish lay dead, and the great auk's strong beak plunged into the flesh and ripped away great chunks which were swallowed in almost an ecstasy of eating.

His belly filled, the big bird marched into the surf and paddled directly south, heading again for Ocracoke Island, part of that long narrow stretch of sand extending from Cape Hatteras to Cape Lookout. That is where his flock would be and his flock needed him.

Bucking the heavy waves, it took him most of the day to get across the sound — a journey that had taken him perhaps no more than five or six minutes when he had ridden in the arms of the great wind. Nonetheless, he enjoyed the tiring swim considerably more than his free ride.

The island was much changed and there was no living thing in sight. He stood high and sent that rolling screech penetrating through the diminishing wind but there was no answering call, no answering movement. The surf pounding the shore here was much heavier than it had been in the more protected waters of the sound, so he did not venture out into it. Dusk was coming on rapidly and his swim had made him uncommonly tired. He waddled to slightly higher ground, hunkered down beside a clump of grass that had somehow escaped the wind, and there he slept.

A piercing shriek awoke him at dawn. His head snapped forward in a cocked attitude and the sound came again from far to the southwest. He answered it in three great bursts of shrill sound and then wobbled off in that direction. The wind was less than five miles per hour now and the sea swells had gentled greatly. He pushed out from shore and soon was swimming swiftly a hundred yards out, parallel with the shore.

He saw them in a few moments — four great auks standing on the shore, their heads thrown back as they voiced their piercing call in chorus. Within ten minutes he had joined them. There was a pathetic, mournful quality about their voices as they greeted him and he stood still and endured with relish the caresses of their beaks over his neck and head and breast.

A gladness welled in the big bird's heart as he recognized one of the great auks as his long-time companion, the old one-eyed female. She seemed tumbled and worn but whole nonetheless, and a chirring chatter trembled softly far down in his throat as he rubbed against her neck.

He looked the other birds over sharply then, but his mate was not among them. He seemed perplexed and shook his head as if to clear it. The flock had numbered one hundred and fifty-six birds. Surely more than just these four and himself had survived the storm. There *had* to be more. He raised his head and the piercing call rolled out again across the emptiness of the seashore. The others joined in and they called steadily for five minutes and then intermittently the remainder of the day. They received no answer.

The next morning the five birds paddled off toward Cape Lookout. The beach there was just as deserted and without trace of the other birds. They turned back toward Cape Hatteras. They swam leisurely now. The smaller fish were returning to the shallows from the deeper waters where they had taken refuge and the birds fed well upon them. Occasionally they still sent out the screeching call, but the intervals were farther and farther apart as they consistently met with no answer.

Four days after leaving Cape Lookout, the birds came ashore at Cape Hatteras. Here they gravely inspected the upside-down carcass of a large dead horseshoe crab, poked curiously at a shiny green corked bottle until they had set it adrift and then probed in the sand with their beaks for moon snails and little mollusks.

Several desultory hours were spent in this manner and then, in one swift movement, all five heads were lifted high. Far, far away a sound was barely audible in the light breeze. Twice more it was repeated and now there could be no doubt as to its origin. The throats of these five birds swelled and that trilling roll sounded forth in a great trumpet call. Far to the north one of a pair of very large black-and-white birds stood high on the water and flapped a pair of ridiculous little wings.

The five remained where they were, but their eyes never left this approaching pair. Within twenty minutes the arrivals coasted through the small breakers and waddled onto the beach. There was a long, crooning reunion.

Both of the birds were females.

One of them was the great auk's mate.

X

THERE were only seven of them.

Throughout the weeks that followed the reunion of the two with the five, the birds were constantly alert for the arrival of more of the great auks. No more ever came. These seven were the last. These seven were the remaining hope of their species. It was a frail, faintly flickering hope.

There was some luck in this number of survivors, for of the seven, four were last spring's fledglings — two males and two females — and would pair off for breeding when the time came. The great auk, of course, had his mate. This left only the old one-eyed female who had now been alone for many years and would always remain so, yet who was somehow closer to all of them than any one other bird. She was, in some strange way, the binding thread, the vital spirit that linked them all and willed them to carry on. The great auk was the leader, but the old female was somehow more than this.

The loss of the great majority of the flock in the hurricane was a tragic occurrence but it was not necessarily the final blow. There was still a chance for increasing their numbers if the spring migration could be completed safely. From these seven birds could come three offspring the first year, at least three the next, possibly six or more the year after that. Slowly, steadily, with great good fortune, their numbers might flourish again — for the individual birds could live more than thirty years and could reproduce for twenty of these. Perhaps with a benevolent hand from nature and no further interference from man they could spark a new population which would equal or even surpass their former numbers. It was unlikely, true, but so long as a spark of life burned within them, they would try. This is the unalterable law of nature.

The winter passed casually and it seemed that once more Nature had gathered them under her mantle of protectiveness. It was more difficult, of course, to herd a school of fish with so few birds — but then, by the same token, there were not as many bellies to fill and there was never any difficulty in getting enough food.

The great auk did not explore the beaches this season as he had done during his first year down here, but he watched with slow-blinking, approving eyes as the young great auks delighted in discovering just those things that had so thrilled him.

Sometimes for days at a stretch he would stay by himself, catching his fish in a solitary manner, content to be alone and sleep on the sunny sand when not feeding. There were other times, however, when he became decidedly gregarious and swaggered through the flock barking quick little commands and hustling to and fro to make certain they were carried out. There were days when only he and the old one-eyed female were together, swimming far out in the sea or waddling along lonely beaches, and, equally, there were times when he was inseparable from his mate.

As winter progressed and began its waning into spring, these latter moods for companionship with his mate became more and more pronounced and for long hours the two would stand side by side and stare toward the north as if waiting for the vagrant wind to bring the call.

Then, in early March, the call came. The great auk felt an exciting stirring deep within himself, an over-powering obsession to start swimming and not stop until his great splayed feet marched up the inclined rock ramp of his own Eldey Island. There was no doubt in him now that this is where they would go. He knew the rest would follow and he knew it was a good place to go, where their hatchlings could be raised in peace and safety.

He stretched high on his toes and his wings beat

rapidly until they were a veritable blur and their slapping on his sides was like the drumming of a ruffed grouse on a hollow log. His beak pointed toward the heavens as that thrilling, booming roll issued from it and the other birds stared at him in admiration. Slowly the call died away, the wings stopped their flapping and he dropped back solidly on his feet. He shuffled through the firmly packed sand to the water and entered it without looking back. He knew they would follow.

In moments the old one-eyed female had moved up beside him, while his mate swam on the opposite side, slightly back from them. The other four swam without concern for order, constantly changing position, here and there diving and having a generally marvelous time of it all.

Three times before, the great auk had been past this shoreline and the landmarks were now wholly familiar to him. Here they passed the last of the great savannah grasses. Now they came to the vast bays, the Chesapeake and the Delaware. Far from shore they surged past the heavily populated areas where boats were as thick as ducks on the water and the men were even more numerous. Here was great Long Island where the old female's mate had been slain so long ago.

By mid-April their sure and steady strokes had carried them beyond that long beckoning arm that was

Cape Cod and into the churning spring surf of New England. Because they were making good time they spent one full day dawdling, sporting with schools of shad and capelin along Maine's craggy coast and climbing onto rocks to cast themselves into the water either with a hearty splash or with scarcely a ripple, depending upon their mood.

They fed well, preparing themselves for the much greater hardships of the remainder of their journey across the frigid Labrador Current and far into the North Atlantic to Iceland. At one point they waddled upwards to a rocky outcrop two dozen feet above the heaving water and here they spent their first night on shore since leaving Cape Hatteras.

As the sun shot its first rays across the rippling surface, the birds stirred, shook themselves and chattered softly to one another. It was time for the big swim to resume . . . but they had lingered too long. Seventy feet away two heads peeked cautiously over a ledge, then disappeared.

"Y'see," hissed a large man excitedly to his smaller companion, "I tol' you they was auks. Them's the big'uns, too! Collector fella in Boston's offerin' twenny-five dollars fer ever' big auk you bring 'im. Lordy, ain't we lucky, though. I ain't seed none of 'em in years."

"Seven of 'em there," the other whispered hoarsely.

"That's a hunnerd an' sevendy-five dollars. C'mon, let's git 'em!" He started scrambling back to the vantage point.

"Wait!" said the first, grabbing his arm. "Easy! Them critters kin hear a pin drop at twenny yards. We gotta do this careful like. Soon's we shoot, them others'll dive in an' be gone. We on'y got one shot each. We'll have to shoot at the same time. Try an' git one in front of t'other so's you'll git two at onct. Then load up agin as fast as y'kin."

The second man nodded and the two quickly checked their guns. A moment later their heads appeared over the ledge again, this time shoving the two big black-barreled rifles before them.

"Shoot when I say 'now!'" said the bigger man and the other grunted in acknowledgment.

To these men, professional waterfowl hunters, this was the opportunity of a lifetime. Now that these big birds had become scarce certain collectors were paying premium prices for their eggs or carcasses. This pair had no intention of letting that easy money slip from their grasp.

On the shelf the great auk stood on his toes and applauded the sun with his little wings. The others watched, ready to follow his lead and begin the second leg of their migration. Suddenly the thundering shots splintered the air and two of the younger birds fell

to the ledge, one lifeless and the other kicking frantically. The old one-eyed female staggered toward the
rim of the ledge, a red stain spreading on her immaculate breast feathers where a ball had grazed, ripping
away plumage and a little flesh.

The great auk's own right wingtip felt on fire where
one of the balls had nicked him and slightly torn the
skin. The five instantly launched themselves from the
ledge and disappeared beneath the green waves.

"Got two of 'em!" the big man bellowed and the
two men scuttled across the treacherous rocks on all
fours like a pair of fantastic crabs. The big man
reached the downed birds first and picked up the
young male, who was still kicking. Quickly he brought
his gun barrel down on the bird's head and the kicking
ceased.

"Them others dived in," commented the other man
glumly. "Reckon we'll see 'em agin to shoot?"

" 'Spect not," grunted his companion. "Onct them
fool birds dive, they're gone. They kin swim better'n
two miles 'fore they gotta come up fer air."

"Well, watch close," said the other, apparently
accepting his big friend's exaggeration as fact.
"I think I hit two of 'em an' if one of them what
jumped in is shot up, he may not stay under so
pretty long."

Six fathoms below the surface the five great auks

swam desperately toward open sea, wings pumping in perfect harmony with the rubbery feet. From a distance they looked like some strange school of fish. Seven minutes later and a quarter of a mile from the fateful rock, the quintet surfaced. Back on the ledge the men looked deceptively small and ineffectual at this distance.

Now they were five. Both a male and a female of the younger birds had been killed back on the rock. Still, that left two pairs to bring new chicks to life and start the great auks back on the road to recovery. Had there been a choice, they still would not have given up in despair. Of course, there was no choice. As long as they were alive, they could not give in.

On they surged, day after day, past the Bay of Fundy, still giving a wide berth to Cape Sable, up the long coastline of eastern Nova Scotia, through Cabot Strait and into the Gulf of St. Lawrence.

The water was cold. Colder, in fact, than the great auk had ever found it at this time of year — and the farther they progressed northward, the colder it became. Following Newfoundland's rocky west coast, they skimmed through the Strait of Belle Isle and rounded the hump of Labrador. Here they spent one day fishing in the coastal waters, filling their stomachs with rich, oily fish to sustain them during their perilous drive across Davis Strait. The passage was made safely and on the twenty-third day they skimmed around the point of Greenland's Cape Farewell.

Now they were in an area of dimly remembered horror and they stayed far from the fiorded shore for five days, traveling almost due north. The waters here were filled with plankton and the blowing of whales and porpoises became commonplace.

They headed almost directly east on the morning of the sixth day along Greenland's east coast, and the knowledge that they were on the last leg of their journey back to Eldey Island filled the great auk with a vast excitement.

Occasionally flocks of birds flew over them and croaked cheerfully at them. Fly they might, but no other bird of the North Atlantic was as swift or as strong on the water or under it as the great auk. But the power that had made them the swimming wonders of the northern bird world was also responsible for the school of black-and-white monsters who caught sight of them shortly after they started eastward.

They were masters of the sea, these twelve, their huge, viciously toothed jaws fixed in perpetual rapine grins. The great auk was familiar with these creatures, for they were killer whales of the same type that had devoured his own father.

In view of their insatiable appetites, one would think these killers would scarcely deign to glance at the five birds — all of which could hardly whet the appetite of one of them. But this day the hunting had been poor and the threads of hunger tugged at them. When they saw the birds, the hunt was on.

At nearly the same time, the great auk saw several of the black, six-foot-high dorsal fins slicing the water toward them like dreadful scythes and he screamed a hoarse command.

If the speed of the birds had been impressive before, it was phenomenal now. Their only chance lay in returning to the shallows where not even the killer whale would follow lest he be smashed against jagged rocks by a relentless sea or collide with them during a headlong chase from which he could not stop or veer in time. The water churned behind the birds and they sped along the surface faster than a man can run . . . but not fast enough.

The old one-eyed female, still weak from the shot that had grazed her breast in Maine, lost her strength and was soon outdistanced by the other four. When the latter were still seventy yards from the shore, the water beneath her suddenly erupted. A huge killer whale snatched her on his way up. He cleared the water completely — and by the time he struck the surface again, the old female had been swallowed.

The great auk screeched another command and the remaining four dived. Their only hope now was to hide among the craggy rocks below and carefully make their way to shore. The great auk and his mate veered slightly to the north while the pair of young birds headed straight for the island. The latter pair never reached the bottom. Beneath the surface they could pretty well out-maneuver these great beasts individually and scoot away in time to avoid their brutal rushes, but three great disadvantages were working against them — there were a full dozen killers in the herd, the birds' air supply was considerably more limited than that of their adversaries and, finally, they were already extremely weary from their long swim.

A dozen times several of the killers made passes at them and each time they slipped away, but they were still far from the bottom and their air nearly expended from the frantic exertions. The pair panicked and shot toward the surface and were lost. Still thirty feet down, one killer caught and engulfed the male, nearly catching the female at the same time. The female veered past those great jaws and straight into the cavernous mouth of another.

The great auk and his mate, meanwhile, had reached the security of the rocks on the bottom and carefully picked their way from one dark grotto to another until they, too, felt the desperate need for new air. Ahead they could see the blessed sanctuary of a rock climbing from the murky bottom and ending over them in a swirl of silent foam, indicating it protruded from the surface.

Swiftly they winged and kicked their way toward it. The female's lead increased as the great auk's injured wingtip slowed him. When they were still four fathoms from the surface a killer spied them and torpedoed to the attack. Quickly the female swept out of the water and scrambled up the slick rock.

Only scant feet from the surface the killer's mouth opened wide to snatch the great auk and in that final instant the bird swerved sharply to the left. The jagged teeth of the monster raked across his back and the impact threw him a dozen feet out of the water. Wildly flailing the air he crashed into the jutting rock, slipped, then clung desperately and slowly, painfully inched himself up toward his mate ten feet above the water.

Below them in a dazed circle swam the killer, its head bleeding profusely from where it crashed into the rock in its eagerness to catch the great auk. Listing to one side and only a few feet below the surface, it headed back out to sea.

For two days the pair of great auks remained on the shore of this vast island that had brought them so much grief and now had proved their salvation. Because of the slash across his back, movements were difficult for the great auk, and the female caught numerous fish for him. They would have done well to stay there for a week or more, but the call of Eldey Island was too great and on the third morning, after a long careful look at the sea for killers, they waddled into the water and left Greenland behind them.

There was an element of great courage in the way these two stately birds — last of their entire species — resolutely headed for the nesting ground. Still there was that nebulous shred of hope that they might be able to perpetuate their race. This, after all, was the purpose of their existence.

Almost immediately after leaving the shoreline, the birds ran into dense, cold fog which persisted for days, and now, for the first time for both of them, they encountered icebergs — tremendous islands of blue-white ice floating freely with the will of the North Atlantic currents. They passed almost within the shadow of several of these floes. As the fog finally lifted they saw the ocean here was heavily dotted with them.

An extremely large berg less than half a mile ahead abruptly tilted to one side and then thundered completely over, filling the air with a great roaring and spawning a huge wave which the birds rode over easily. The wave caused something of a chain reaction, however, for as it struck dozens of other icebergs, it caused two more of them — both smaller by far than the first — to topple and turn turtle in a similar manner. Wisely the birds no longer passed the icebergs at close range.

It was a difficult swim to Eldey Island for the great auk. He had traveled this span of water between the island and Greenland only once, and that time it had taken seventeen days. The gash across his back was ugly and hampered his movements so badly that it was twenty-three days before they caught their first glimpse of the island.

They had traveled at a steady slower-than-moderate pace without stopping and as the first rays of the sun climbed over the horizon, they saw far ahead on the water a pillar of fire capped with dark smoke; and the great auk burst out in a delighted screech at the sight. There it was, Eldey Island — Fire Island — and he was coming home at last after two full years. He was bigger and certainly wiser, with a jaw that could never be exactly right again and a wingtip injury that was healing wrong and a terrible wound across his back, but he *was* still in one piece and he was coming home!

With their three-thousand-mile swim almost over, the great auk dipped his proud black head as if in deep approval of the sight of his island and permitted a grating note of triumph to escape the thick beak. The cacophonous thunder of ten thousand bird voices smote their ears and it was a delightful sound of welcome to them. They glanced about to see the puffins and razor-billed auks, dovekies and murres, guillemots and skuas and half a dozen others flashing through the air over them or riding the swells over near the islands. It was a wonderfully happy home-coming.

Just as he had learned to do on this same spot two years ago, the great auk rode a high swell onto the sloping rock shelf and this time his mate was by his side. When the swell receded they waddled forward toward higher ground, past the bunched masses of innumerable birds of all varieties squatting over their eggs or lurching toward the cliff edges to throw them-selves into the air or water. Swiftly, despite the pain from his back wound, the great auk led his mate to-ward the same spot where he was hatched. Unfortu-nately, it was occupied by a pair of exceedingly belligerent razor-billed auks who had no intention of giving it up.

Higher and higher they climbed with an increasing urgency within them, and then, almost at the very summit of Eldey Island on a rounded promontory, they found a wide flat ledge unoccupied. They claimed it as their own and now they were home in all respects. As they had the previous year on the treacherous plateau of Danells Fiord in Greenland, the two great birds mated once each day for six days. The only difference now was that the great auk did not move about or fish as much as he had then. An inner instinct told him he must not move too much if his back were to heal and he must get well quickly in order to help feed his mate and offspring.

The open salt-washed gash slowly became a scab-encrusted sore and the almost constant pain of it slackened; the fire of inflammation disappeared and soon he would be well and whole again.

Below the great auks on all sides stretched a blanket of birds, mostly murres. Here were clustered a mass of cormorants, there a great patch of guillemots and a few scattered groupings of razor-billed auks, but always there seemed to be an incredible murre population in all directions.

Most of the birds below them already straddled eggs, for it was late May now. It was time for the female great auk's egg to come and, when it did, it was the largest on the entire island . . . and the most handsome.

It was an incredibly strong-shelled egg. This was essential, for no easily breakable egg could long have lasted on those bare rocks where the ever-probing wind delighted in rolling them about and bumping them roughly into nearby rocky prominences.

The egg was as big as a man's fist and, like the

eggs of the murres, tapered sharply almost to a point
so it would roll in a circle on the flat rock and not
plunge off the ledge into the water or onto jagged
rocks below when the wind touched it. Unlike the
soft green-and-brown-speckled color of the thousands
of murre eggs below them, the great auks' egg was a
rich creamy white with occasional spots of bright
cinnamon brown, with a scattering of deeper burnt-
umber splotches.

Fate has seldom been more capricious than on that
third day of June when, in the early dawn light, a
sturdy three-master anchored in the hazardous waters
a short distance from Eldey Island. A single boat was
disgorged and it carried six men and three boys. It
was a difficult and dangerous business to land on this
island that had such a strong reputation for disaster
among Icelandic mariners. It was chanced this time
only because the vast bird populations of the other
more accessible islands nearby had been so preyed
upon by meat and feather hunters that now the only
island with a profitable population of murres and
guillemots was Eldey.

After several unsuccessful attempts to tie the boat
to shore in the smashing swells, the men solved the
problem by pulling it clear of the water on the very
sloping rock used by the great auks.

When the boat was secure, the men strode toward

the crowds of nesting birds with shouldered clubs. It
was a terrible, all too familiar picture unraveling
before the eyes of the two great auks high above.
Frightened, but not enough to leave their eggs, the
smaller birds below watched the men approach them.
Even had the murres become severely alarmed, they
could not have fled, for they were too close together
to run and they could not take to air from level
ground.

As the men drew perilously near, the murres bowed
low and then bobbed up and down rapidly, their
breasts sometimes nearly touching the ground. From
thousands of throats came a great thunder of *"Errr!
Errrr errrr! Errrr!"* riding the whipping wind.

Quickly now the men pushed into the midst of the
nesting murres and the blunt clubs began rising and
falling. The three boys, not yet in their teens, who
had disembarked with the men, ran back and forth
among the dead birds gathering the greenish eggs and
occasionally throwing them at one another with glee-
ful laughs.

When one of the men paused for a moment to
remove his hat and wipe the sweat from his brow, he
glanced from the murres and his eyes followed the
promontory upward, only to widen in disbelief when
he spied the huge forms of the two great auks staring
solemnly down at him.

"Garefowl!" he screamed. "Garefowl! Garefowl!"

The other men stopped their grisly work and followed the line of his pointing finger and their mouths opened in surprise and pleasure. Here, indeed, was a fine bonus!

Swiftly the six men spread out and climbed the promontory, advancing on the two great auks with their clubs ready. The two birds watched their approach with mounting apprehension. Finally, when the men were only twenty feet away, the great auk screeched a command and he and the female scrambled through the tightening ring as rapidly as they could, but they were on land now and their movements were sluggish and awkward.

As the female darted between two of them and headed for the cliff edge a bloody club streaked down in a vicious arc and crushed her skull. She was dead before her body stopped rolling.

The great auk managed to elude the swings of two men and then was hit a glancing blow by a third. He rolled over, scrambled back to his feet and continued his pitiful wobbling run toward the cliff edge. The men rushed in pursuit — and one of them, intent only upon the great auk's fleeing form, stepped on the single large egg and crushed it into an obscene yellow stain on the gray rock.

Only a dozen feet separated the great auk from

the edge now, but it was too much. A whistling blow from a club slammed into his neck and shoulders, shattering bones and stopping him permanently.

The man picked up the great auk's broken body by one wing and looked it over. The feral pleasure on his face quickly dissolved and was replaced by a deeply etched scowl.

"Aaagh," he growled to the others, "wouldn't you know that would be my luck? Look at that great big sore on his back. Probably diseased. Nobody would want to eat that meat and I couldn't even sell the hide with that thing on it. Just my rotten luck!"

Carelessly he tossed the great auk's body away and it rolled to a stop near the edge overlooking the rest of the small island. The man who had killed the female slung her over his shoulder by a leg and the party trooped back down to slaughter more of the nesting murres.

Above them, body shattered and neck broken, the great auk's fierce brown eye retained a dimming spark of life. The carnage continued below him until thousands of birds that had been standing in a blanket all over the island were dead or had finally taken alarm and fled. The small boat made several trips to the larger ship with its cargo. Every murre egg had been stolen or destroyed and only the eggs of the dovekies and puffins, hidden in their clefts and crannies and burrows, had escaped unscathed.

The pitiable voices of the surviving birds were a chorus of grief as they flew around the tragic little island or paddled confusedly in the water a short distance away.

At last the little boat and its men were lifted into the mother ship and they disappeared around a shoal of distant islands, heading for their home port on Iceland's Cape Reykjanes.

The great auk did not see them go. A film had formed over the once bright eyes and the rapid heart-beat slowed. At last, with the cries of the injured and anguished birds still ringing in his ears, he closed his eyes for the last time and released a final wheezing breath.

The great auk was dead.

Epilogue

O<small>N</small> June 3, 1844, on the island of Eldey, also known as Fire Island, off the southwestern coast of Iceland, the species of a large penguin-like bird known as the great auk became extinct from the face of the earth. This occurred when the last two living specimens were killed by Jon Brandsson and Sigourour Isleffson and the egg of these two birds was smashed by Ketil Ketilsson.

Sixty-two years later the great naturalist and explorer Charles William Beebe wrote:

"The beauty and genius of a work of art may be reconceived, though its first material expression be destroyed; a vanished harmony may yet again inspire the composer; but when the last individual of a race of living things breathes no more, another heaven and another earth must pass before such a one can be again."

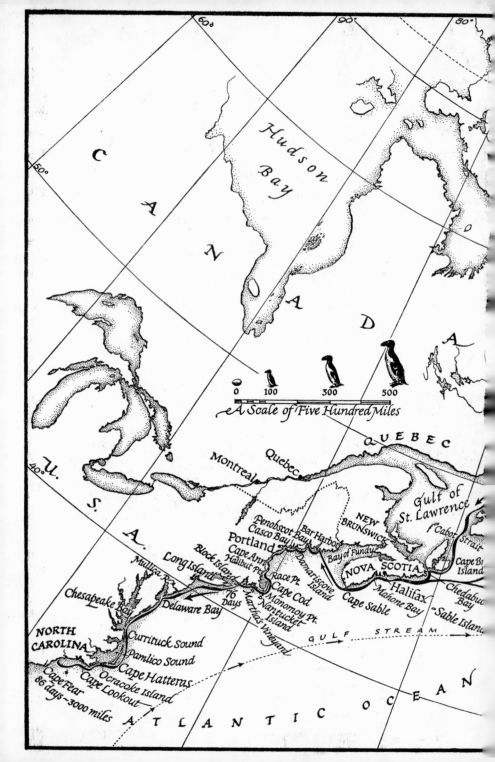

60°

90°

80°

Hudson Bay

C

A

N

A

D

A

50°

A Scale of Five Hundred Miles

0   100   300   500

QUEBEC

40°

U.

S.

A.

Montreal

Quebec

Gulf of St. Lawrence

Cabot Strait

NEW BRUNSWICK

Penobscot Bay   Bar Harbor
Casco Bay
Portland   Damariscove Island
Cape Ann
Halibut Pt.
Block Island   Race Pt.
Long Island   Cape Cod
Monomoy Pt.
76 days   Nantucket Island
Delaware Bay   Martha's Vineyard

Bay of Fundy

NOVA SCOTIA

Halifax

Cape Breton Island

Chedabucto Bay

Cape Sable   Mahone Bay

Sable Island

Chesapeake Bay

Mullica Bay

NORTH CAROLINA
Currituck Sound
Pamlico Sound
Cape Hatteras
Ocracoke Island
Cape Fear   Cape Lookout
86 days ~ 3000 miles

GULF   STREAM

ATLANTIC   OCEAN